the Weir

AND OTHER STORIES

the Weir

AND OTHER STORIES

BRIAN MILLARD

Published 2023
by Workshop Publishing

ISBN 978-0-473-66658-3 (Paperback)

Designed and distributed in New Zealand by The Copy Press, Nelson, New Zealand.
www.copypress.co.nz

CONTENTS

The Weir

Birmingham England 1928

Diary entry April 1.

I will soon be officially a spinster of this parish, a dried up old maid, still a virgin at thirty. I console myself by reading Marie Stokes' manual 'Married Love' secretly in the privacy of my bedroom. During the day I keep it well hidden from prying eyes. It would not do to have Mom or any of the youngsters find it. Marie Stokes seems to understand how I feel, she proposes a new model of 'companionate marriage' and urges men and women to discover a loving sexual intimacy with each other. The old ideas simply have to change. April Fools Day today and don't I fit the bill perfectly?

Diary entry April 3.

How can I explain what foreplay is to Harold? He would think I had gone completely off my trolley. He's just like all the other men of his generation in this town, who believe that women are only here to give them pleasure and provide a receptacle for their seed. A woman's job from then on, as far as they are concerned, is to give birth, cook their meals, do housework and care for their children. Well they will have to wake up, things are changing elsewhere in the world, we have the vote now, we have jobs, It might be a little late for me to become a flapper but I am not dead yet. My goodness, if you told your average Brummy male that a woman is capable of orgasm he would not believe you, probably fall off his bar stool laughing and spill his beer. So Harold, it's time to show what sort of man you really are. Dare I give him 'Married Love' to read?

Ethel had never strayed far from the nest, was still the dutiful daughter, biddable and obedient on the whole, accepting of her mother's pretentiousness and authority without question. She was always willing to do household chores and abide by the teachings of their church to which they were both unfailing members of the congregation.

She had a good job as a warehouse checker. She was well liked by her co-workers and the bosses. But her vivacious personality veiled a strict moral code. Her faith made her utterly honest, trustworthy and tolerant of the failings of others. If she disapproved of inappropriate behaviour at work she made no comment and simply turned her back to it. There had been many men who had asked her out and others who thought they could take advantage of what they considered her naivety and gullibility. They had found themselves wooing a brick wall. There was another Ethel, possibly several, all locked away safely like a collection of Russian dolls, one inside the other. The outside version, the one exposed to the world, clung fiercely to the Victorian ideal and was a model of propriety. Yet inside, growing impatient to spread her wings, literally flap like a bird and express the new freedom and liberation, was another Ethel. It was this Ethel who was the problem. She was capable of creating chaos. So much so that in trying to repress this inner self Ethel might feel faint, even in need of smelling salts. Often she was obliged to take to her bed until the episode passed. A couple of years earlier she had suffered a complete mental breakdown when her moral code was challenged and she had found herself in two minds regarding a relationship with a perfect rogue of a man who had charmed and almost

Brian Millard

succeeded in seducing her. During his fondling of her breasts she had heard quite clearly the voice of the preacher and her mother warning her of the terrible consequences of copulation outside of marriage. The young man had produced a rubber thing he had purchased from a vending machine in a public lavatory and proposed to use it. She had felt horrified but curious, torn between the desire to experience what she had denied herself all her life and the fear of the consequences. It left her with guilt and confusion.

On one hand she considered the Lord had saved her from a dreadful fate, yet the inner Ethel had told her she was a fool and she was throwing away her life. This simply contributed to her unresolved feelings of guilt. The ensuing depression and fatigue that followed saw her under the care of the family doctor who offered no diagnosis, other than stress and did not disclose what he suspected, which was that she was experiencing a female condition, formally recognised and published in the Lancet journal, called 'female hysteria'. Treatment was possible and had become popular, even fashionable in the rarefied realms of the gentry. However the doctor was sure he could not recommend such treatment for Ethel as it involved manual massage of the pelvic and genital areas.

In fact, Ethel had been experimenting in a similar manner for some time. When drowsy with sleep or when besieged with lewd thoughts, she had attempted to use the means literally at hand. The problem was, even though this could produce intensely pleasurable sensations, it also invariably created an all consuming sense of guilt, for which Ethel believed in her heart she deserved to be punished. It was followed by the all too familiar feelings of depression and self loathing which could culminate in a mental breakdown.

Ethel began keeping company with a young man called Harold Alcroft, a quiet unassuming fellow, also deeply religious and a year her junior. Harold was an electroplater earning a good wage and had prospects. Ethel was quick to spill the beans to her mother who was equally quick to ask to meet the young man. Harold was promptly invited for a meal. As far as her mother Mary was concerned, her thirty year old daughter could do a lot worse.

Her not so subtle probing into his family background and earning capacity provided enough positive information for a nod of approval. Even if he was not exactly welcomed as a member of the family immediately, Harold was made to feel at home and he and Ethel began seeing each other, more frequently, somewhat formally but on a regular basis. There was little physical intimacy, not because Ethel rejected any advance but because Harold was one of the world's rare true gentlemen, he had no wish to pressure Ethel in such a manner. Things would change if the day should come and they married. He would wait until that day came. He was steady and predictable and most certainly a good catch. If Ethel found him boring it was something she would not admit to herself or anyone else. It was not long before Harold proposed formally and was accepted.

Ethel's Diary: Thursday July 14th 1930.

A cinema has opened in Perry Barr, all very modern and smart. I saw the program for the inaugural film show in the Despatch. The architectural design is in the Moorish style both inside and out. I have told Harold he must take me to the opening double feature, they are both talkies, 'Illusion' with Charles Buddy Rodgers is a romantic comedy, and the other is Stewart Rome in 'Dark Red Roses' a drama. So there will be something we both will enjoy, I hope.

I realised the other day that Harold and I have been keeping company for more than eighteen months, how time has flown.

Diary entry Sunday July 17th 1930

Harold is utterly reliable and absolutely trustworthy. Mum continues to approve which is amazing but she is concerned he might jilt me at the last minute. I doubt the thought has ever entered his head or likely to. He took me to the new cinema

Brian Millard

last night. He enjoyed 'Illusion' as much as I did. It was all about a vaudeville magician, played by Buddy Rodgers and his assistant, played by bubbly Nancy Caro. They are a close professional team and physically attracted to each other. Then typically he becomes infatuated with a snooty socialite and almost breaks poor Nancy's heart. As it turns out Nancy is nearly killed in a motor car accident. It brings Buddy to his senses and of course everything turns out well and there is a happy ending. When the part about the accident happened and Nancy is in hospital, Harold held my hand. He is such a dear boy, he brought along a box of expensive chocolates and I almost scoffed the lot.

The other movie, Dark Red Roses was OK but scared me a little, Harold was petrified, my turn to hold his hand. It was all about this sculptor whose wife takes a lover who is a pianist. When the truth is revealed, the husband, in a jealous rage tries to chop off the pianist's hands. Harold by then was almost under the seat and I had no option but to comfort myself with the remains of the chocolates.

Mom wants me to invite Harold for supper on Friday. Most of the tribe will be elsewhere, Dad, banished to his lair and only the younger siblings allowed to attend on condition they don't interrupt the adults or they will not get to eat one of Moms shepherd's pies so early in the week. Something is up. I can't think what it is but Mom is definitely up to michief.

Diary entry Monday July 19

Last night I had a fit of the giggles. During the meal Mom was particularly charming and attentive to Harold, insisting he take second helpings of shepherd's pie and literally spoon feeding the poor fellow with apple crumble even after he had complained he had eaten more than enough already. Then she tried to ply him with Dad's special bottle of port. He of course is Tee-total and simply refused point blank to imbibe. I felt really sorry for him but could not help seeing it as funny. Mom was insistent, almost chasing him around the table. She finally gave up and then asked him point blank what his intentions were and if a *marriage date was drawing near? He looked at me with his eyebrows raised and his hands turned palm up, not knowing what to say, looking for guidance from yours truly. All I could do was shrug and say 'Soon?' to which Harold grinned his stupid grin and said 'Well yes, soon, very soon. This appeased Mom to some extent although she was obviously not completely convinced because no actual date was forth coming from either of us. She had no alternative but to appear satisfied. She excused herself and went off to bed leaving Harold and me to clear away and to wash up the dishes. Poor Harold, it could not have been much fun for him as he was clearly embarrassed. I must find a way to make it up to him.*

Diary entry Wednesday July 22

I've thought of a way!

Ethel was in the kitchen the following Saturday peeling a mountain of King Edwards for the midday meal. She had something to tell her mother and she was not sure what her reaction would be. Mary came in from the garden bearing a massive cabbage and a bunch of freshly pulled carrots. Ethel had the kettle on the hob in preparation for making tea. She took her mother's arm and sat her in a chair. 'It's time for a cuppa Mom. Put your feet up for a bit. There's something I need to tell you.'

They were on to their second cup when Mary said, 'Out with it my girl, I know when you are up to something. Is something wrong between you and Harold?'

'No Mom don't talk daft, everything's just the same. It's just that I have holiday leave that needs using up and I was talking to my friend Vera about nice places to go to and she told me about her honeymoon in Bournemouth in Dorset. It sounds a really smashing place. There's a big theatre called the Pavilion just been built, she went to see a play there and she said it was ever so good. She and her hubby had a lovely time. Anyway she gave me the address where they stayed in a very fashionable area. She said the accommodation was excellent. So I've made a booking. I wrote to the lady who owns the house and she wrote back to say she had just the two available vacancies. I know I probably should have told you earlier but I had to make a quick decision, so I did.

Her mother did not know how to respond, 'Two vacancies?'

'Yes Mom, a room for me and the other for Harold, a week beginning the second of August. We will go down by train.'

'I see. Was this Harold's idea?

'He doesn't know. I haven't had chance talk to him about it yet. He may not even want to go. He'd better though or I will forfeit the deposit.'

Mary was torn between propriety and the hope that this development might bring a wedding closer,

'Then you had better tell him, hadn't you? Just remember you are not Mrs Harold Alcroft yet.

'Oh Mom, Who do you think I am?'

'It's not you I am worried about.'

At this Ethel burst into laughter. 'You can't be serious. We *are* talking about Harold?'

Diary entry Saturday 25th July

Harold did not appear terribly enthusiastic. I expected him to be concerned about taking a week's holiday together but he barely said anything, just stared at me goggled eyed as if I was suggesting we elope to Gretna Green. So I told him that should he refuse it would be the last he ever saw of me. Of course he had to agree in the end, even pretended to be keen but I knew he wasn't. He did offer to pay for half of the accommodation. I refused but suggested he book and pay for the train journey.

Who cares what other people think and what his church cronies will have

to say? If he doesn't pull his socks up and take the lead now and then, he will certainly lose me. I made it perfectly clear. So we are off to Bournemouth one way or the other. I am not sure what the fashion is now with bathing costumes. I will ask Vera if she will lend me hers.

Bournemouth was everything they hoped, the weather when they arrived was perfect, the guest house clean and inviting. They had rooms across the hall from each other and comfortable single beds. The landlady was polite and business like. As she was showing them their rooms, she had made a point of mentioning that it was a respectable establishment with a set of rules. These were printed and pinned to the wall near the door in each room. The list gave details of the normal services, also a warning that the front entrance would be locked at 11.30 each evening. Any guest wishing to gain entrance after that hour should borrow a key from the proprietor before going out. Last but not least, prominently displayed in bold type were the words. 'This is a God fearing establishment. We do not condone intimate fraternisation between the sexes outside of wedlock.' The landlady drew their attention to the list of rules before wishing them a happy stay in Bournemouth.

Diary entry Sunday 2nd August

Harold and I are finally in Bournemouth. It seemed an interminable journey from Snow Hill. But the scenery was wonderful and changed from one vista to the next. As we neared Masbury the steam engine struggled to get to the top of a very steep length of track. Apparently we climbed to eight hundred and eleven feet above sea level. Harold had been reading about the railway line and bored me stiff with all the facts he has absorbed. I got soot in my eyes, which was most uncomfortable. I can quite understand why they refer to this train-line as the 'slow and dirty' and the 'slow and doubtful.'

Brian Millard

The guest house is lovely. It is in Wellington Road and most salubrious. We plan to do a spot of exploring before the evening meal which we had to order in advance. There are other guests here, we nodded and smiled at a couple as we arrived. I can't wait to see the sea close up. You can smell the ozone from here with the bedroom window open. Harold has relaxed already and is resting in his room, the poor man insisted on carrying most of our luggage quite a way from the railway station.

Later Sunday

We walked all over the town. The new Pavilion Theatre is very grand. The theatre can seat five hundred and would you believe the ballroom can hold up to a thousand. The gala opening was only last year and the Duke of Gloucester came from London in a special train for it. They attract all the top musicians and performers, so lots of people from all over come to Bournemouth just to see a show or listen to a concert with Prima Donna opera singers and so on. The building overlooks the sea and out across the Pleasure Gardens to the white chalk downs of Purbeck Ridge. Harold's maps and guide books are in constant use! He says he will take me to a concert this week. It makes me so happy when he shows he really cares. But in truth I would love to go to the ballroom and dance until I drop and then maybe Harold will scoop me into his arms and make passionate love to me? Oh dear more wishful thinking. Bought a few postcards on the grand tour- a picture of the Pavilion for Mom and Dad, a couple for the rest of the tribe showing the beach and a few bathing beauties and a saucy one for Vera and the girls at work which has an illustration of a very busty lady in the sea, and an onlooker with his eyebrows raised. The caption says 'Nice pair of water-wings lady'. I must find time to write them and post them in the morning.

We had booked an evening meal at the guest house so raced back to be on time. The meal was not too bad although some of the other guests seemed rather reserved. I nodded and smiled anyway. We walked our feet off today and so turned in early in preparation for a day on the beach tomorrow. I have just this moment finished unpacking. I think I have caught the sun already. Harold pecked me on the cheek very chastely and disappeared into his own room a few minutes ago, I feel sometimes as if he is afraid to actually touch me.

Diary entry Monday August 3

Well wonders will never cease. We spent almost all day on the beach today. Vera's bathing costume fitted me perfectly, in fact a little too well. It showed off a few curves I never knew I had. I just lay on a towel and listened to the waves and soaked up the sun. I am paying for it now as my shoulders and legs are surely burnt. Harold ran to and fro fetching refreshments each time I asked. Amazingly he even agreed to stop wearing his best suit on the beach, it seemed so déclassé sitting there sweltering, with his shirt sleeves and trouser legs rolled up. So after a little nagging he actually purchased a one piece costume. It is rather tight fitting and has bold horizontal stripes. He went off to a changing shed and emerged posing like Charles Atlas, flexing his biceps. He was most embarrassed because he ran into the waves and leapt about pretending to dive in and so forth and no sooner did the costume get wet the shape of his manhood became clearly visible. So he spent most of the time trying to cover the offending appendage. At least he agreed to change out of his suit. Like me he can't swim for toffy.

I am working on him gently to take me dancing. He claims to have two left feet.

On Tuesday Ethel awoke feeling unwell. Perhaps it was the exertions of the day before and the sea air? For whatever reason she was definitely off colour, But she had no intention of wasting a second of valuable holiday time, so when Harold asked how she had slept she answered with 'Can't complain.' However when she felt nauseous and unable to eat a bite of breakfast, she had to admit, at least to herself, the truth, she was undoubtedly in the early stages of her old malady. She was able to summon enough energy a little

 Brian Millard

later to accompany Harold to the beach, post her postcards and sit in a deck chair as Harold paddled and eventually waded out into the slight surf and played the fool trying his best to cheer her up and lighten her mood. Sadly his efforts were in vain. Ethel claimed to feeling dizzy and needed to lie down. Harold gathered all the things they had brought with them for a day at the beach and trudged back to their lodgings, stopping every ten minutes for Ethel, at snail pace, trailing behind, to catch up.

Back in the guest house, things took a turn for the worse when Ethel began to behave oddly. It was as if she had withdrawn into herself and, for no apparent reason, would begin an earnest conversation with no one in particular, then giggle at nothing, intermittently demanding to know if anyone still had any love for her. Each time Harold tried to reassure her, she smiled in a resigned sort of way then burst into mirthless laughter, as if it was all a big joke. Then abruptly she stood, announced she was going to her room, 'To have a little nap before our next exciting excursion.'

She reappeared less than an hour later asking if he had any plans on how to spend the rest of their time in Bournemouth? Harold attempted to ignore her obvious sarcasm and suggested she spend the rest of the day in bed and he would wake her for the evening meal. Later he knocked on her door and told her supper was being served. She told him to go away, she wasn't interested in food. Harold offered to bring her meal up on a tray. 'Do as you wish,' Was the response.

Diary entry Wednesday

Oh God help me. I feel incredibly sensitive down there and dare I say in need of Harold's touch not mine. 'If he really kissed me properly, I would offer myself to him without hesitation. This feeling has been building in me now since we arrived in Bournemouth, Harold must see what I need. It can't be a sin if you truly love someone. The feeling is over powering. I could not eat supper last

Ethel closed her diary and zipped it into her small travel bag. She lay on her bed, got up again and undressed. She washed in the wash basin on the chiffonier, dried herself and went to the chest of draws in which she had folded her underwear and nightwear. She found the special night gown she had purchased as part of her trousseau. It was sheer and revealing, intended specifically for her wedding night. She put it on, brushed her hair and looked at herself in a cheval mirror. Silently she opened the door to her room and peered along the hall. She took the few steps to Harold's bedroom door quickly and knocked on it. Harold's door remained closed so she tried again more assertively. She looked about her, fearful of anyone appearing and seeing her 'in flagrante delicto'. But the door opened and there was Harold in his striped pyjamas, his hair wet and a towel around his neck. He looked at her, rubbed his eyes with a corner of the towel and took another longer look. Before he could form a word Ethel took a step towards him and throwing her arms around her neck propelled him back into the bedroom, kicking the door too with her foot. 'I just wanted to say goodnight,' she said, kissing him on the mouth, holding him tightly and pressing her body to him. She had dreamed of kissing as passionately as this but in the dream it was the man kissing her and she feigning resistance. But she persisted and felt Harold respond in a similar passionate manner. She was amazed to feel his member harden against her thigh. But then Harold broke free of her embrace, pushed her away and held her at arms' length.

'No, no Ethel we can't. We mustn't do this. You must go back to your room. Think of the repercussions should we let this go any further.' He opened the door poked his head out, there was no one there. 'Go now,' he whispered, pushing her through the door and closing it firmly.

Ethel, dazed and utterly deflated at what she considered Harold's callous rejection and bewildered by her own stupidity, staggered to her bedroom, collapsed on the bed and burst into uncontrollable tears. She felt as if her heart had been torn from her body. The hopelessness of her situation undeniable, the guilt and remorse unbearable, she wept and continued to weep until exhausted, she could weep no more. Her eyelids closed and she allowed the familiar dark depression to wrap its black cloak around her.

Diary entry Thursday.

This is more than I can bear.

On the Thursday morning having slept very little, Ethel arose late, washed her face and brushed her hair like an automaton. She looked pale and drawn, not a glimmer of light in her eyes. She considered going back to bed but decided perhaps a little sea air might improve how she felt. She went downstairs to find Harold polishing off scrambled eggs on toast. He offered to get her the same and helped her into a seat. He poured her a cup of tea apologising for having started breakfast without her and explained how he had thought it best to let her sleep on. He made no mention of the incident of the night before.

'Well what would you like to do today? He said brightly. She looked at him blankly. 'How do you feel about a gentle stroll along the pier? What do you think, are you up to it? It was as if she had not heard him. Harold leant across the table and took her hand. There was no response. 'Whatever is the matter love? Ethel. Please answer.' He looked around the dining room apprehensively. It would not do to make a scene here. He shook her shoulder gently 'Ethel what is it? What is wrong? Come on now, don't be this way.' He shook a little harder.

Ethel had withdrawn to a safe place within herself, she looked but did not see, was indifferent to words. Harold's pleading did not immediately register. It was only when his touch became more insistent did she feel herself being shaken reluctantly back into harsh reality. She raised her head and met his eye. Harold smiled sympathetically, 'So what do you think? Another breath of Dorset sea air might do you the world of good. There are plenty of things of interest we have not seen.' He suddenly remembered about the Pavilion Theatre and the ballroom. He had made a promise to take her there. 'We should see about going to the Pavilion as well. Would you like to go on Friday night, it will be our last chance?' Ethel nodded and tried hard to smile but instead tears welled up in her eyes. 'Now then, there's no need to get upset. It's not the end of the world is it?' He went to the tea urn and came back with a warm cup of rather stewed tea. He found Ethel recovered enough to nibble half heartedly at a slice of cold toast on which he had spread for her a generous amount of homemade marmalade.

Ethel still listless and with no interest in anything at all, allowed herself to be cajoled and led along the pier. Nothing she saw or did engaged her interest. When asked a question she seemed unable to formulate a sensible response. Other couples on the pier were promenading, a profusion of boaters and parasols giving the pier a festive air. Other couples were having fun, eating ice cream, shopping for mementos, some spooning, all happy to be by the sea on a glorious day. But Ethel, listless and non communicative was not completely there to take part. At the Pavilion she made no comment when asked what she would like to see or do. She simply shook her head and did not reply.

They wandered around the centre of Bournemouth aimlessly and finally boarded a tram heading north. It did not matter where it went but Harold, almost at his wits end was desperate to find some way of shaking her out her sullen mood. The tram went to a place called Winton. Winton had little to recommend it. It was a quiet little country village not yet geared to take advantage of the tourist trade. It was only one mile from Bournemouth. Even before they got there Ethel became dizzy and in danger of falling. She kept demanding the tram stop and let her off. A kindly lady passenger asked if she was alright. She put the back of her hand to Ethel's brow and looked earnestly at her. 'Young man,' she said, 'you should take your wife to a doctor.'

'No,' she cried. 'No doctor, no doctor.'

There was no alternative but to go back to the boarding house as soon as possible. Harold half carried Ethel from the tram and they sat on a bench until it returned from its terminus.

When they were back at the boarding house Harold helped her to her room, asked again if he should locate a doctor. He would enlist the help of the landlady. At this Ethel became hysterical and demanded he leave her alone. Fearful of other guests hearing her raised voice, Harold retreated to his own room and then went down stairs to read the local newspapers. He periodically went back upstairs to check on her but each time he tapped on her door and enquired if she was alright, she told him to go away.

When he decided to go to bed, he made one last attempt to speak to her and wish her goodnight. But there was no reply. He opened her door peered in and realised she was not there.

He was half way down stairs when he encountered the landlady on her way up. 'My fiancée, have you seen her? She is not in her room.'

'Oh, I think I saw her go out about half an hour ago. I thought it a bit late for a stroll. She did not ask for a key.'

Now becoming worried and unsure what to do Harold decided to look for her. It was now quite dark, the streets virtually empty. When he saw a couple walking towards him, he described Ethel and asked if they had seen her. They shook their heads and walked on. Harold combed the town, he went to every place they had visited, walked the beach. At the tram terminus in the square a man asked him if the last tram had left. He also had not seen Ethel. Harold replaced his steps, peered into doorways and dark places. He had no alternative but to go back to the guest house, telephone the police and report Ethel as a missing person. Nothing could be done until the following day. They requested he drop by the station in the morning should she not appear. He was assured she would come back soon. Harold could not sleep that night. He went over endlessly what had preceded her disappearance. Had he been wrong in rejecting her? How could he have done what she obviously expected? How could he have taken advantage of her when she was so obviously behaving irresponsibly? Most men would not have hesitated and then cast her aside afterwards. Surely she could see it had been in their best interests for him to have refused. Where had she gone? What if something unthinkable had happened to her? When it grew light Harold washed and shaved then retraced his steps again as the town began to stir. He went back to the Guest house and had breakfast. Ethel had not returned and Harold was by now desperately worried.

Ethel had simply left the guest house and walked away. She had no particular destination. She just put one foot in front of the other and walked and walked and continued to walk. It was almost dark. She had walked south blindly for more than an hour and when she found herself in countryside she rested for awhile. Her long skirt and small jacket kept her warm enough. She had brought no money or sustenance with her, so she sat in long grass and listened to the silence. She thought she could hear water. She stood and walked towards it. Soon she could hear it roaring angrily, she walked on, drawn towards it. Soon the noise, accentuated by the stillness and silence of night, seemed deafening. Ethel felt her ankles grow wet, the coolness of the water refreshing. She had no fear and purposefully waded towards the sound of the river.

When her skirts and petticoats billowed around her she was faintly amused. She was suddenly buoyant, her skirts with air trapped beneath them, supporting her. She floated, enjoying the sensation, she lay back allowing the current to take her where it wished, her arms flung wide in supplication. She was drawn close to the source of the roaring by the fierce current. She closed her eyes, a smile on her lips, content. Then she began to move faster and faster, circling the eye of an underwater whirlpool. For a brief moment

 Brian Millard

a flicker of reality may have entered her mind, as she was dragged under, into a black void as dark as a grave.

On Friday evening another visitor to Bournemouth walking along the river Stour near the Throop Mill Weir saw Ethel's body in the water. He promptly informed the police. He and PC James Brewster together recovered Ethel's body. It was taken to the mortuary to await an inquest.

When Harold was questioned he said he had been keeping company with the deceased for the last nineteen months. He related how she was a jolly girl but at times became very depressed. She had suffered a severe nervous breakdown about five years ago. They had come to Bournemouth on the second of August and until Tuesday she was in the best of spirits and appeared to be enjoying herself. Then she became dazed and listless and did not seem to grasp what was said and began to behave strangely. On Thursday he had insisted she see a doctor but she refused. Later that day she was 'all of a shake at times and acting rather queer.'

Harold explained how he had taken her to her room at eight thirty and told her to go to bed. She said she would, but at nine fifteen he learnt she had gone out. He went in search of her but could not find her. He then reported the matter to the police. As far he knew she had no worries of any kind and they always got on very well together. He suggested that due to her not knowing the district she may have attempted to walk across the fields and so went into the river. Dr G.M. Brooks said he was satisfied the death was caused by asphyxia due to drowning and a nervous breakdown was a contributory factor.

On Saturday the ninth of August, Ethel's death made head line news in the Bournemouth Daily Echo. It shared the front page with an article reporting the success of the Australian cricket team led by Don Bradman in the first Home Counties match in Northampton.

The Humane Killer

For the boy it was the best of times. The days seemed crammed with new exciting adventures. He would walk for miles along railway tracks, stopping now and again to listen with his ear to the track, he believed it was a good way to hear if a train was coming. But steam trains gave plenty of warning and so the theory was never really put to the test.

He did his fair share of trespass and stealing, taking stray eggs from where the hens had laid them in the cows' stalls was a regular favourite. He was almost caught once but managed to push a few eggs into his trouser pockets and under his shirt, only to fall and break them all and ending up covered in egg yolk. He became adept at finding the biggest mushrooms, some were massive. He would chase, and now and then catch, ducks by the pond but could never hold on to one for long. He would climb into farm machinery and squeeze between threshing spikes and cogs. If a button had been pushed or a lever turned he would have ended up as mincemeat.

In the kiln the farm labourers would leave big stone jars of cider. He and his sister would help themselves, inevitably he was caught. He must have been more than a little drunk because he was not as nimble as he normally would have been and could not run away. To teach him a lesson, a big farm worker hung him out of the hayloft door at the top of the kiln by his braces. He dangled there at the mercy of his trouser buttons until the labourer deemed it punishment enough. He was quite good-natured about it but the boy did not touch his cider again. Danger of one form or another was not far away in the country.

He would spend hours beating his way through nettles and rubbing their stings with dock leaves for relief. He would come home laden with plums and huge cooking apples. He would bruise the apples deliberately to make them more palatable. The lanes were very leafy. The foliage so thick it was like walking through a tunnel, the hedges comprised of intricately woven branches of hawthorn laden with berries and swags of nuts. He would count the milestones on the way home to their cabin. Wildflowers were everywhere.

There was an abandoned piece of antiquated farm machinery alongside the duck pond next to the cabins. It was probably some kind of outmoded harvester. It had a wide flat roof which kids used as a stage to perform 'acts' for the adults. He and his sister tried to do a sand dance which they had seen performed at the Hippodrome by a couple of funny men dressed in striped nightshirts and red fezzes. It was hilarious at the theatre but the children had no sand, no striped nightshirts or a fez between them, so they improvised and did a Charleston instead, the bit where you open and close your legs and your hands go which ways. His sister, always a show-off, performed her acrobatic dance routine, which culminated in her tucking her frock into her knickers and doing a backbend.

The families ate together in the big shed and cooked on the open fire in the large hearth. There was a violent thunderstorm one night and a drenched black lamb appeared outside. It was brought in to be near the fire and wrapped in a blanket.

There was a pair of Shire horses to pull the dray used to transport the big sacks of hops. He was allowed to hold the reins. There was little need to try to steer them in any direction because they knew exactly where to go. If their tails went up it meant they would fart or drop a load of horse shit. His sister would crack up when they farted.

One horse was called Barney, and if the horse broke wind the drayman would snap the reins and say, 'Barney, you bloody bleeder,' and the horse would snort or whinny as part of the joke.

Whenever they saw Barney, even if it was at the end of the day and he was grazing in a field, they would chorus 'Barney, you bloody bleeder'. His ears would flick up and he would react in the same manner.

They were also friendly with a few pigs kept on a neighbouring farm. In the main room of the farm house there were sides of beef hanging from the rafters and hunks of bacon being smoked in the chimney. On one visit they fed the pigs a few apples they had stolen.

When people they did not know began to arrive and congregated outside the cottage, waiting expectantly, the children were mystified but curious, so hung about as unobtrusively as possible. A shooting brake with wooden trim drove into the farmyard and a few of the local people started to gather around it talking quietly. The man in the brake unloaded several odd bits of equipment, amongst them an impressive set of scales and a leather case of other implements.

To their astonishment the pig they had just fed with an apple was dragged into the yard by the ring in its nose and tail screaming blue murder. Half a dozen men held it still and the man from the shooting brake walked up and placed what looked like a starting pistol to the pigs head and shot it between the eyes. The boy learned later that the gun was called a 'Humane Killer'. The man then calmly slit the animal's throat, catching most of the blood in several buckets. By then the boy and his sister were glued to the spot, too shocked to move. When it seemed there was no more blood forthcoming, the man nodded and twigs and straw were piled up all around it and set alight. When the fire died down the pig's outer hair had been completely burnt off. The ashes were scraped away and a few willing hands scrubbed the pig clean.

The butcher was offered beer but declined. His next job was to dismember the carcass which he proceeded to do with great economy. The pig was placed on a wooden gurney. The butcher opened up his leather case and selected a variety of knives and set to. He first disembowelled the animal, the guts spilling out and caught in a container. Each organ, as he separated it from the carcass, was weighed and carefully placed in a white enamel bucket with a lid. Soon the bucket was full and then was another. Before long the pig had been reduced to so many different cuts of meat. The whole process, horrific as it was, was conducted with dignity and almost with reverence.

As the afternoon wore on, all that remained of the animal was a large membrane stretched to dry across two branches of an oak tree. Their mother, coming to find where her children had got to, found them looking at the membrane, wondering what it had been and what it might be used for. Sausage skin seemed to be the answer. It was about then that his sister started to bawl her eyes out and the boy began to reflect on the casual way life can end.

Brian Millard

It happened one night

On his first day of duty at the Cambridge Military Hospital, in the Casualty Department, he was given a key and a tape measure and told to go to the mortuary and measure the length of a body he would find there. The mortuary was really a little chapel hidden in the grounds of the hospital. This was his first posting and he had been recently promoted to corporal to match his new responsibilities. He wanted to please.

He went into the mortuary and there on a slab was the body of a soldier. His jaw was taped, his nostrils plugged, and he wore a shroud. He was definitely dead. He prodded him in the shoulder with his finger to make sure. He had never seen a corpse before. He measured him and found he would have been a little over six feet tall. He left, gave the warrant officer back his key and told him the measurements.

'I thought they might be something like that,' the warrant officer said and grinned. It had of course been some kind of initiation.

On another occasion a couple of Horse Guards came in off the street. And stood waiting in reception. One of the Horse Guards was missing his lower lip. His mate explained how his horse had bitten it off.

'Where's the lip now?' The corporal asked. It was not very far away so he gave the Horse Guard a sterile plastic container and sent him off to find the missing lip. The lip was found and came back in its container. It was promptly sown in place. It was to grow a little crookedly but was fine.

On the same day there was a road collision involving an Army truck carrying troops, standing holding to whatever they could find, in the back. The truck had overturned. A burly soldier carried his injured mate in over his shoulder. His mate was examined and attended to. Whilst this was happening, the corporal observed the soldier who had carried the injured man change colour and sink into the seat in which he had been waiting. It turned out he had a ruptured spleen. He had actually been in a great deal more trouble than the mate he had carried over his shoulder so effortlessly.

Then there was the regular soldier with long service but with a history of depression and frequent suicide attempts. He was often admitted and saved from death at the last moment. He had tried various ways of ending it all but had been foiled every time. He finally hit on the idea of simply not eating or drinking. He was admitted looking like something out of Belsen. He was force-fed but resisted. He was drip-fed intravenously but tore the tube out of his arm. He died. It was the ultimate example in 'dumb insolence'. He must have figured he had beaten those who oppressed him and won some sort of victory. He certainly was defiant and determined.

The young corporal had become accustomed to riding in an ambulance to disasters of one kind or another. There was an incident when a civilian lorry driver had died at the wheel. He had managed to stop the vehicle before expiring. The corporal and an ambulance driver drove out to pick up the body. He was a huge man and they struggled to lift him on to a stretcher and into the ambulance. They took him to the hospital mortuary and were asked to undress him prior to an autopsy. The ambulance driver took the full weight, straddling the corner of the slab awkwardly between the dead bloke's legs and grabbed a fist full of shirt. The corporal took hold under the armpits. They lowered him onto the slab. 'He's a big bloke,' he said. 'Now let's have a go at his trousers. Just think he dressed himself this morning.' One arm of the dead lorry driver flopped over the corporal's shoulder, a hand with tobacco-stained fingers and bitten nails dropped under his nose. Do you ever get used to this?' he asked the ambulance driver.

'No mate,' Replied the driver. You don't.'

In the Cambridge hospital in the nineteen fifties, medical officers were reasonably relaxed about formalities. There was very little saluting, and officers rarely pulled rank. QAs, short for Queen Alexandra's Royal Army Nursing Corps and particularly sisters were not always so approachable. No doubt the nurses were on their guard and suspicious of the intentions of any soldier who tried to be friendly. The sisters or senior nurses could act officiously.

The corporal had become friendly with a couple of nurses. In fact, he had made a date with a nurse to go to the pictures in Aldershot to see 'Giant' starring James Dean, Rock Hudson and Elizabeth Taylor. He had to agree to take and pay for her friend to come as well. It was not a successful date. The attractive Scottish girl, on whom he was keen, turned out to be an obsessive pincher. If he got anywhere near her, she pinched him hard. Just accidentally brushing her arm elicited a pinch to the ribs. He bought both girls an ice-cream. In the dark he leant across his date to give her friend an ice-cream, and his date gave him a huge pinch that made him drop the carton of ice-cream in her friend's lap. He did not think they liked the film or him and before the end of the movie his date announced that she and her friend were on duty in half an hour and they had to get the bus back. He felt obliged to leave with them. He saw the end of the film many years later. When he examined himself in the shower block next morning he was black and blue with bruises. He could see the shape of her viciously sharp nails about his ribs.

He was a little more successful with a very good looking if considerably overweight nurse whose acquaintance he made when he was on night duty. Night duty was rostered sometimes week about but more often monthly. It was not too bad except for the problem of lack of sleep. Trying to sleep during the day whilst a company of soldiers was being drilled outside the window of the dormitory was almost impossible. Those coming in and out of the billet also had little concern for someone trying to sleep, so after a week of night duty, he was past being tired. But this particular QA made it worthwhile.

Whenever it was possible he would keep her company in her cubicle beside her ward. They would converse quietly so as not to disturb her patients. He learnt she was an 'army brat' and had spent her life travelling from one camp to another before becoming a nurse. Her father had been a colonel, and now was retired. The family home was in the Surrey countryside. She was able to visit her family at weekends. These illicit encounters were not without an element of romance. Occasionally they touched briefly, more correctly she touched him, put her hand over his and once accidently brushed his shoulder with an ample breast. He had hopes of further intimacies but that night his reverie was interrupted dramatically and brutally.

A Hermes aircraft returning from the Middle East, carrying seventy passengers, fifty of which were Army families, and twenty three RAF families, under-shot the runway at Blackbushe Airport in Hants. The plane burst into flames.

The corporal was alone in the Casualty Department and answered the call from the airport alerting the hospital to prepare for a possible emergency. There was a standard procedure to be followed. The corporal made the calls he was required to do and soon there were people coming into the hospital, rubbing sleep from their eyes and making preparations for a disaster. He was on good terms with the sergeant in charge of the ambulance drivers and had frequently attended accidents with him. So when the sergeant came in with his drivers, in the small hours of the morning and still dark outside, it seemed not unusual. The sergeant and his team were ordered to Blackbushe without delay. Soon the hospital was as alive as on a regular day. In next to no time the casualty team had been roused and readied itself.

Sharing his duties in Casualty was a little OXO cube of a Scotsman from the Gorbals. Although not very tall he was built solidly. He was called 'Butter', not because he was soft but because he had a nasty habit. If someone was in range, he would try to 'butt' them. A person was wise to stand well back when attempting to converse with him. It was probably an involuntary, built in action he did without thinking. Apart from this minor

 Brian Millard

problem Butter was a good man in a crisis. The head nurse liked him, as did most of the MO's, but then he may have managed to control his urge to butt any of them.

Word was received from the ambulance crew. Many more ambulances would be needed, also personnel and stretchers. The only place at such short notice which had vehicles of any kind available and conscripts to drive them was an Ordinance Corps training camp nearby. In short order, raw recruits, having been ordered from their beds were dispatched to the scene, driving armoured vehicles of all types from the camp.

The first ambulance arrived back at the hospital. The face of the sergeant was black with soot and anger. He came into the reception area fuming.

'What stupid prat sent fuckin' recruits who've only been in the Army for five fuckin' minutes? He shouted in his thick Scouse accent. 'No training, wet behind the fucking ears, all of 'em. They are back there picking up body parts. He grabbed hold of the corporal and said 'Come on mate gimme a hand.' The pair of them went to the ambulance and came back carrying a stretcher on which there was the still smoking body of what once had been a soldier.

'Poor bugger croaked before we got 'ere.'

The other two ambulances arrived. More victims were carried in on stretchers, the remnants of uniforms smouldering, the smell terrible. A tall, normally happy go lucky medical orderly, dragged from his bed, and not quite awake, took a look at what was on the stretcher and vomited in a corner. Lying on the stretcher was a staff sergeant with no face. He had no ears, no nose and no hair. He had no extremities at all. His mouth, without lips, seemed to be fixed in a grin. His teeth set against the red of what was left of his face, looked artificially white. His eyes were like fried eggs. They carried him and two others into Casualty, and a little later two more arrived in the same condition. There was one who was not so badly burned. The corporal and Butter helped cut away the remnants of uniforms and did what they could. Two died within twenty minutes. The others, now looking like mummies, bandaged from head to toe by the senior nurse and another QA, were eventually wheeled into a ward and placed into oxygen tents. Only one survived the week. The corporal finally got back to the dormitory and tried to sleep.

It was touch and go for several weeks for the surviving young officer. But after months in an oxygen tent and extensive plastic surgery, he eventually recovered enough to be able to converse with the occasional visitor. During one of the weekly visits the corporal made to see him, he learnt, listening with his ear close to a slit in the bandages encasing his mouth, that he had been the first to get out of the plane. He had been sitting next to the exit and had opened the door. He was on his way out but turned around to help a little girl. He got her out safely and decided to go back again to help others but then there was an explosion.

He was eventually allowed to exercise outside in the hospital yard, his wounds repaired well enough for him to join in kicking a football around the compound with his head still encased in bandages.

When an epidemic of Asian flu swept the country, suddenly the hospital was admitting flu cases by the hundreds. Within a couple of weeks every ward was full, and patients were spilling out into the corridors. The hospital was working at full capacity day and night. URTI (Upper Respiratory Tract Infection) became the most common diagnosis on a chart.

By the time the epidemic had run its course many of the hospital staff had contracted Asian flu as well. The corporal was not spared and also had to be admitted. As it happened he was placed in an available bed in the ward of the QA with whom he had become acquainted. He had been ill for almost a week before she appeared on night duty and he was well on the way to recovery.

On her first night, as she did her rounds, she said, 'I'll see you later.'

He waited, wondering what she had in mind. When it seemed the other patients were asleep, she slipped out of her office, came to his bedside and pulled a screen around the bed.

'Take those off,' she murmured, tugging at his pyjama bottoms. 'I'll just be a minute.'

He did as instructed and waited expectantly.

She came back and whispered, 'Lie on your side.' She pulled back the sheet, patted him on a buttock and gave him an injection of penicillin.

As I said to Cubby

The Sunnyside Retirement Village offered no end of leisure activities. There was, for instance, a well used swimming pool in the basement of the community centre where once a week a lithe young female instructor led a group of residents in keep fit water exercises. It was a common sight to see groups of grey haired residents in bathing costumes, some wearing rubber hats and goggles, hanging on to inflated plastic tubes, moving in unison, attempting to emulate the instructor in front of them. And then on the ground floor, adjacent to the reception area of the centre, there was a billiards room, and next to it a small cinema, plus a restaurant offering reasonable three course meals for about ten dollars and cask wines for three dollars a glass. There was also a modest library, a communal reading area and a medical centre with a resident nurse on hand. A glassed in balcony over-looked a manicured bowling green.

The residents of Sunnyside retirement village were, in their way, a microcosm of NZ society and reflected a broad spectrum of personal life experience, skills and interests. A variety of organised societies and clubs catered for groups sharing a common interest. Some groups were more formally structured than were others and had, in typical Kiwi fashion sprouted committees with individuals voted as chair. As such is the nature of any society or organisation, the more dominant individuals had their acolytes and either by accident or design were surrounded by less dominant members of the group. As in all groups of people there are usually hierarchies and amongst the ageing residents of Sunnyside there were very few who did not follow the status quo. The majority of residents, having determined to make the most of the rest of their lives, had little desire to take on responsibility for anything if it could be avoided. There were others who paid lip service to any form of authority yet pretended to go with the flow. 'Rocking the boat' is a term harking back to the first colonial settlers. A vessel bound for foreign climes was usually crammed full of strangers. The passengers soon learnt that to be 'divisive' was not a good idea. The Sunnyside Retirement Village could be likened to such a vessel, as can the vast majority of New Zealand.

By the time a couple decided that their needs had changed, the husband, as a rule, was not the man he may once have been. When they are ready to relinquish the pressures and stresses of a world which may appear to no longer have any further use for them, and when they consider their home to be too big and too expensive to maintain and the time has come to 'scale down', it makes sense to add to retirement funds from the proceeds of selling the family home. A retirement village then, more likely than not, seems the sensible option.

But once the move is made, the wife as a rule finds it easier to make new friends than does her husband. She fits into the group or groups on offer more readily. In any event in a retirement village there are normally fewer single male residents than single women. Many women adjust to the life style more readily than do their husbands. Most of them will survive their husbands. As one might expect, the Sunnyside Retirement Village had its fair share of loud, self assertive older ladies as a result.

Sam Calloway had been a resident of Sunnyside longer than most. Sam was not a physically big man but this was deceptive. He projected, in his dress and manner an aura of the English Edwardian gentleman, courteous, and faintly effete. He was in fact the product of Cambridge University where he obtained his medical degree. His previous working life had been in New Zealand as a nephrologist in private practice. He was quietly spoken, and this could be mistaken, erroneously, for a diffident disposition. It belied the pragmatic intellect of a man who held his own counsel and possessed a mind as sharp as once was his scalpel. His life had changed dramatically when his skills and medical expertise became needed in a more domestic role. His wife bizarrely suffered kidney failure. By then he had reached retirement age and so was content to spend his days tending to his wife's needs. They had no children. He purchased the latest dialysis machine and set it up with other equipment in a spare bedroom and this they called the surgery. He was able to monitor his wife's condition closely and adjust the schedule of transfusions as required. Sam kept his wife alive for many years and nursed her until she died.

It was then Sam decided the time had come to move on. He bought a chalet in the first stage of building of the village, virtually off the plan. Since then he had watched the expansion and the growth in residents with interest. He was by nature gregarious and made friends easily. But after ten years in the village he had seen many of his friends succumb to one disease or another and either die or been forced into private care. Within the resident community a pragmatic view and acceptance of the inevitability of death was the norm. To be taken at the end by pneumonia, generally called 'the old man's friend', was desirable as it was considered to be a less painful way to go- better than lingering and being a burden to others. A fatal heart attack fell into the same category. Sam was acutely aware of the natural attrition in older residents and how quality of life diminishes after the age of ninety. So when it was discovered that one of his older chums was not asleep in an armchair in the reading room but had in fact passed away quietly without anyone at first noticing, it was almost a cause for celebration. To depart the scene so painlessly and gently was thought to be literally a stroke of luck. A new resident moved into his chalet shortly afterwards and soon became one of Sam's friends. He was a Kiwi born fellow called Dennis and there was no doubt Dennis was very much alive and kicking.

At seventy three years old, Dennis was still a fine figure of a man. He carried his six foot three frame well, with a seemingly military bearing. He wore his full head of hair longer than was fashionable and this together with an almost too white smile gave him the debonair appearance of someone in the arts. He wore his jacket in the Italian manner, over his shoulders. It seemed Dennis had once been something in the film and TV industries, (or so he claimed). His stories of the people with whom he had come into contact whilst working for many of the British film and TV studios, from the fifties through to the late seventies, were never ending – some found them beyond belief. He would often refer to 'dear old Dickie' (Attenborough) or 'Johnny' (Gielgud), Larry and Vivian, Sir Carol Reed, Lindsay Anderson and other famous film directors and producers from Alexander Korda to Cubby Broccoli as if he had been on intimate terms with them. He gave the impression that he had been the confidante of film stars such as Margaret Lockwood, Patricia Rock and 'Dear' Liz and Richard- these were amongst the names that fell like snowflakes, dropped casually in the wind.

Dennis had apparently worked his way on a passenger ship to England as a young spark and somehow got into RADA. He was modest about his credits in acting, claiming he was better on the other end of a camera or filling any of the myriad job titles that roll up the screen at the end of a film. He rattled off names of films and personalities with whom he had been involved without gathering breath. 'Dear Johnny (Mills) such a lovely chap, we got on famously when we worked at Elstree Studios in the early days. This of course was after Douglas Fairbanks sold the studios and Lew Grade took them over in the fifties. I worked in most of the big studios. I became quite friendly with dear Peter Cushing when we were together at Hammer Studios. You could get away with murder in those days, with, let's face it, dreadful over acting, shonky production values. But they don't make stars like that anymore. Most of them had a theatre background and had switched from one to the other. I mean take Sir Alec (Guinness), and Dicky Attenborough, well he was a fine looking fellow in his youth, and quite the lad, if you take my drift? Moira Shearer was a lovely girl. I can remember after a wrap, we all got on the turps…well that's another story.'

     Brian Millard

Dennis it seemed had broken into films when his physical resemblance to the actor Stewart Granger was noticed from a casting photograph and this led to employment as his stand- in.

Dennis would relate how he had made the move to television shortly after ITV began in the British Midlands in the sixties. The list of programs and shows in which he claimed to have acted, produced or directed, were legion. That one man could have been involved in them all, defied belief. Dennis was certainly larger than life. Yet he was engaging, intriguing, liked, admired by some. There were detractors who considered him a blowhard and poseur. But whatever the truth may have been, Sam liked him. He saw his lust for life and his depth of experience as a stimulating asset to the village community and so was happy to call him a friend. What did it matter if he had or had not been more than friendly with Margaret Lockwood or Joan Collins? Sam was generous enough to take it all with a grain of salt.

Perhaps partly due to Dennis's general level of fitness, he displayed prowess on the tennis court and in particularly on the bowling green. So much so, that in no time at all, he became the skip of the bowling team. He proved to be a generous but firm leader adept at devising strategy and tactics. He certainly looked the part in his impeccable whites, snappy Panama hat and silk cravat. Whether he really knew what he was doing or he was simply acting the part, it did not matter. To observe him engrossed in the action as if he was directing a film, sitting, one leg thrown nonchalantly over the other, his linen jacket hanging over his shoulders and his finger tips touching his lips in contemplation, before gathering the team together and revealing his master plan, was reassuring and stabilising.

Sam had already become a respected member of the team. Over the years he had developed a degree of skill that was enviable. He had never played the game before he came to Sunnyside. In fact he had never been very good at any organised game. Bowls had opened a door for him. He looked forward to dressing in his whites and wearing his bowling hat. In a match, when it came his turn to bowl, he approached the task with all the finesse and seriousness normally displayed on an operating table. A look would come into his eyes and his demeanour was no longer that of Mr Nice Guy. He would take his time to sum up the play, the positions and the lie of the 'land'. Only when he was absolutely sure his calculations were correct would he send his bowl curving seductively down the green, It might kiss an opponent's bowl seemly lightly, yet send it reverberating out of play, then on the rebound his bowl would connect gently with a teammate's and nudge it into a winning position near the jack. On rare occasions his tactics might be dramatically different. When there was no alternative, he was capable of delivering a devastating dam buster and bringing the end to a close with his bowl jack high. As a result Sam was often used as a surprise deadly weapon, held back until the final end and usually winning the day. As permanent fixtures in a 'fours' team – Sam, Dennis, a chap called Bruce an easy going, retired chiropodist as lead and fourth place taken by an ex farmer's wife called Sandra, they were soon playing in tournaments at away matches against teams from other retirement villages. One of the small fleet of people-carriers owned by the village was used to carry the team and a few keen supporters to these engagements and the games took on a new degree of seriousness. Dennis organised the fixtures and arranged for return matches.

He also started up a film appreciation society, showed selected films which were discussed and criticised after the viewing and also gave him opportunity to regale a captive audience with his anecdotes and stories. With Dennis involved life at the Sunnyside Retirement Village was rarely dull. A ménage of what he called his Merry Widows were usually in attendance, vying for attention and hanging on his every word. Sam had little time for any of them considering them generally ill mannered and presumptuous. They followed the bowls team like blue rinsed sedentary cheerleaders.

The Merry Widow's noses were put firmly out of joint when Dennis at one particular away match was observed apparently paying court to a female resident of the opposing retirement village. He at one point, during the break

 Brian Millard

for lunch, was seen to be deeply in conversation with an attractive, obviously cultured lady. They were talking animatedly, breaking into laughter now and again and obviously enjoying whatever they were discussing. When Dennis stood, took her hand and squired her over to meet the team, the Merry Widows fell silent. Sam stood and was introduced.

'Lois I would like you to meet my friend Sam. Sam this is Lois, we go back a long way. Would you believe it, we were at RADA together, amazing to find her here in NZ after all these years. I recognised her immediately she has not changed a bit.'

'Dennis please, you are embarrassing me. It's a pleasure to meet you Sam.'

Sam took her hand and looked into the most beautiful pair of eyes he had ever seen, set in a near flawless skin. When she smiled, embarrassed by Dennis's praise, the faintest of laugh lines about the eyes and around her lovely mouth could be detected but did nothing to spoil her beauty and graciousness. She spoke with a faintly melodious upper-crust English accent, her clear and precise pronunciation betraying her training as an actor. Sam burbled something completely inadequate. She was introduced in a more perfunctorily manner to the other members but not the Merry Widows. Dennis escorted her back to her seat and she pecked him on the cheek. Dennis sauntered back nonchalantly tossing his jacket over his shoulder. Then Lois looked directly at the still transfixed Sam and gave him a smile and an acknowledging wave. The Sunnyside team won the day and a return match was arranged on their home green for a few weeks later.

Sam and Dennis often played chess or simply shared a glass of wine together in the evenings. After one such chess evening when Sam had made a pot of tea and produced a pack of Tim Tams, he learnt a little more about Lois. Dennis had indeed met her at the Royal Drama Academy in London in the fifties. She was then about nineteen years old and Dennis not much more. She was already a trained dancer and wanted to become an actress. Being a dancer explained her poise and the way she held herself, thought Sam. He clearly remembered the tilt of her chin, the way she placed her hands and gestured to punctuate what she said, the grace displayed when she sat in a chair and the way she moved. It seemed she was not destined to become a great actress. Musical comedy and parts requiring dancing were all she had been offered. It was hard working as a performer on stage in sometimes remote locations. Working into the small hours had its drawbacks. Dennis confided he had lost track of her after she married a considerably older wealthy man.

On the day of the return match. The bowls team took their places in the village people-carrier, primed for action. Dennis had given them a pep talk before the transport arrived and discussed what he had perceived as the opposing team's weaknesses. When they boarded the vehicle they were fired up and instilled with confidence. Dennis took his seat next to Sam. During the journey Sam asked him casually if Lois would be there. He was pleased to learn that she would and learnt she was also keen to see him again. He smiled and Dennis raised his eyebrows knowing.

'But I thought you two? Well I assumed…?'

'We are old friends Sam, nothing more…' Sam settled back into his seat, he felt his heart begin to palpitate and had to take a few deep, slow breaths.

The match was a decisive victory for the visitors. Lois had greeted Sam warmly, kissing him on both cheeks rather theatrically. At lunch he gallantly helped her into her chair at their reserved table where she sat demurely between Sam and Dennis. Dennis had ordered a bottle of champagne. They chatted and Sam did his best to appear amusing. He was surprised when Lois laughed, rather too readily, at his efforts.

A few days later she called him wondering if perhaps he might care to accompany her to a concert of chamber music at the University School of Music and perhaps find somewhere Sam liked for dinner afterwards. Sam of course was more than happy, in fact he was delighted. He told Dennis in the strictest confidence of this development and of what could only be described as a date. Dennis simply said 'You old dog, good on you both.' Sam could barely sleep that night.

 Brian Millard

In preparation Sam cleaned his car meticulously. Had his hair trimmed, cleaned his shoes. Lois was supposed to meet him in the foyer of her retirement village apartment block but when he arrived there was no sign of her. He called her on her cell and when she eventually replied seemed to be vague and confused as to who he was and why he was calling. He explained, feeling foolish and disappointed that she had obviously forgotten. She apologised and claimed she had been pre-occupied, there had been a problem with her microwave and the power had only been restored to the building a few minutes ago. She would be right down. She finally appeared apologising profusely. He helped her into the car and drove sedately at the regulation twenty kilometres through the complex and on to the motorway. They spoke of mundane things until they reached Symonds Street, managed to find a park, fed the meter and made their way to the concert hall. Lois, automatically, slipped her arm through his.

This was the first time Sam had been in the company of a woman in this way other than his late wife for many years, yet he felt relaxed and comfortable sitting holding Lois's hand. The young group of musicians filed onto the stage. A conductor appeared, bowed, turned to the group and raised his baton. What followed was a selection of demanding pieces from Vivaldi, Richard Straus, Grieg, Brahms, Shubert and Haydn designed to demonstrate the talents and strengths of the group. After a short interval at which wine was served the repertoire changed to more popular music. George Gershwin, Cole Porter and Leonard Bernstein were featured. Lois clasped Sam's hand when the theme from 'West Side Story' was performed. They both enjoyed the event. This was the prelude to many similarly enjoyable occasions. The following week they went, again at Lois's suggestion, to a talk at the Auckland Art Gallery on Māori Art and culture. They discussed at length what they had learnt and enjoyed. Sam found a new energy. Dennis helped him choose younger and more fashionable apparel. Infrequently Dennis joined them at the cinema and they would go for dinner afterwards, as a threesome. But over time as Sam and Lois grew close, Dennis politely feigned other commitments. In no time at all Sam and Lois were stepping out together regularly. On the slimmest of excuses they would find a reason to meet for coffee. They talked and shared confidences. He grew accustomed to her forgetfulness and often capricious behaviour which he put down to having led a protected and indulgent previous life.

Lois was not overly forthcoming with regard to her background. This reticence Sam interpreted as a desire for privacy and probably a need to spin a little mystery around her past life. When prompted she might hint of trips overseas but often was unable or unwilling to be specific 'Oh its gone,' she would say, rubbing her forehead as if the details eluded her. She had difficulty recalling the names of dates and people, claiming she had always been in a dream, calling it her 'affliction'. Even after almost two years of seeing each other socially, Sam had only gleaned and pieced together the merest odds and ends of her history and still had very little idea of who in fact she actually was and what her present circumstances were.

He *had* learnt that, at the beginning of their marriage, Lois's husband had doted on her, encouraged her interest in dance and given her the freedom to indulge her passion. As a result she was able to cherry pick the parts that suited her. But eventually as she grew older, offers of work dwindled, so she stopped performing. From then on her focus became the supervising and running of the various homes her husband owned. They spent a great deal of time travelling the world together, sometimes for business reasons but mostly for pleasure. At first, they enjoyed a busy social life, she happily playing the part of the charming and attentive hostess, but as her husband's health began to fail and he became infirm, social engagements became less and less frequent until they diminished completely. She nursed her husband lovingly until he died. She had also confided in Sam one evening that she had been the beneficiary of a large proportion of her husband's estate, but maintenance of the properties could not be sustained and so they had to be sold, one after the other. The London apartment overlooking the Thames was particularly valuable and that went first. The proceeds, invested in blue chip shares and commodities, proved a disaster. After the global share market crash she had been almost totally wiped out. She related all this with a bemused air, waving it away as if it had never been of any concern. The country house which she loved – a huge Jacobean farm house set in a vast acreage of mature trees – also had to be sold. It was difficult to sell it for what it was worth. For a while it was let. Various unreliable tenants either defaulted on the rent or damaged priceless furnishing. Then an unscrupulous land agent did nothing to improve its value at auction. And it was sold for a song. The remaining property it seemed Lois still owned but she did not seem absolutely sure, it was of no concern, she rarely used it. The fact that it was situated in a remote village in Scotland precluded regular visits or habitation in any event.

Sam had often felt irritated by what he had at first considered obfuscation, but he came to realise that her vagueness was genuine and not an attempt at being obtuse. Perhaps she had for some reason pushed memories out of her mind and buried them so deep she was no longer sure what actually was the truth or was not. Apparently there was a sister living in Auckland who in her late sixties had decided to move to New Zealand, to be near her and had purchased a house in Epsom. Then her sister died and she was quite alone. It would have been a painful time. She moved again. She bought into the retirement complex on the advice of a friend who already was a resident. In a nutshell, it was all she could or wished to reveal about herself. Sam was no doubt looking for a hint to where she saw their relationship heading–and what she envisaged for the future and what her plans might be. If she had any plans at all she did not reveal what they might be and Sam remained none the wiser. Lois did admit to him that it woud soon be her birthday, although she wasn't sure if she was seventy six or seventy seven. Whichever it was, her birthday would be in a couple of weeks. Sam decided it was worthy of celebration. He would do his best to make it a memorable occasion. He took her and Dennis to dinner.

There was a dance floor at the restaurant. Lois wanted to dance to the piano. She dragged Sam onto the floor. She managed to make him look as if he knew what he was doing and he was happy not to have trodden on her vulnerable looking toes. Dennis then took over. The few other couples who had taken the floor drew back and watched as he and Lois without a shred of pretention proceeded to transport them to another more elegant time. Lois had her eyes closed and seemed to meld into Dennis's body. They were clearly enjoying themselves. They effortlessly gave a joyful, exuberant display of professionalism. When the number came to an end the other guests applauded. The trio drank champagne and toasted the birthday girl. When Sam gave the waiter a nod, the pianist struck up 'Happy Birthday' and the chocolate cake Sam had ordered was produced, the whole restaurant joined in the singing and cheering. Lois was clearly overwhelmed. Sam quite deservedly counted the occasion a success. When it came time to leave he did the old fashioned, gentlemanly thing of helping her out of her seat and noticed a wet stain on the seat on which she had been sitting. Also he could not fail but see a matching wet patch on the back of her dress. He pushed the chair back under the table discretely and said nothing. He felt embarrassed for her. She had wet herself, probably involuntarily. Lois seems oblivious of the fact. Sam was concerned but having no intention of spoiling what had been an otherwise perfect evening, put it out of his mind.

After the age of eighty NZ driving licences by law have to be renewed every three years. A doctor's certificate is required, as is an eye test. The loss of a driving licence spells the end of mobility and independence and can be the fore runner to the slippery slope down into a diminished quality of life. When it had been his eightieth birthday Sam had been lucky that his doctor signed the form he had received from the transport department after only a short perfunctorily examination. But since then Sam was well aware that his eyesight was not was it was and his reactions slower than they should be. There had been frequent lapses in concentration resulting in dings and grazing to his car. He tried not to drive if it could be avoided. In fact, the

 Brian Millard

last time Sam had driven his car, he had to admit that his competence was failing. What happened next was a silly thing, really, but the outcome was embarrassing and expensive.

He had run out of milk and had driven his Suzuki Swift the short distance to the supermarket, parked he thought legally and well within the white lines, in a space outside. He purchased the milk and noticed that a large, expensive vehicle now occupied the space next to his car. It was so close in fact that he had difficulty squeezing into his seat. He began to back out and his wing mirror scraped a deep gouge into the passenger side of the new car. He was horrified and began to panic. He drove forward again and, in the process, damage was done to both cars, he turned the wheel and attempted to back out once more. This resulted in the expensive vehicle suffering even further damage and the Swift losing its wing mirror. Sam sat in the driver's seat with the engine revving, horrified, and unable to open his door. He felt an absolute fool. He was distressed and not a little confused. He could feel his heart pounding and he became short of breath. It took a little while for him to regain a degree of composure. A smart young Asian woman arrived pushing a loaded shopping cart whilst Sam was trying to extricate himself from his vehicle by scrambling over the passenger seat. The young woman immediately took photographs on her cell phone of the scene and of his number plate and car registration. She manoeuvred her vehicle out of the parking space and took close-ups of the damage done to both vehicles. She asked Sam for his name and insurance company, typed the details into her cell phone, put her groceries in the boot and then coolly drove away. Sam drove back to the village very carefully.

The oversized HUV had certainly been inconsiderately parked, he was angry that he had not confronted the owner or taken photographs himself at the time when he had had the opportunity. He determined to make this known to his insurance company when he made the claim. The incident cost him sleep and a great deal of hassle. He had taken his blood pressure when he arrived home. It was considerably higher than it should have been and his heart rate was well beyond normal. It frightened him. Dennis helped him with the insurance claim using his laptop. It would soon be Sam's eighty third birthday and time to again renew his driving licence. He confided to Dennis that he was not looking forward to it.

He took it easy for a couple of days, sat in his wicker armchair in the sun room and read a thriller Dennis had lent him. He drifted into sleep after a few chapters of the Lee Child pot-boiler and dreamt. He dreamt of Lois and her smile.

As it happened Sam's doctor was due for retirement. Over the years the two men had developed more than a patient doctor relationship. During the usual questions regarding his current medication and general state of health, blood pressure and knee tapping, they chatted about this and that. The doctor referred to his computer. 'Have you been experiencing any palpitations? Noticed any shortness of breath?' Sam felt slightly irritated. He did not want to remind him that he checked his vital signs periodically himself and in his own opinion the minor irregular heart beat the doctor had noted at his last visit was nothing serious and had not been repeated. He lifted his shirt and said pointedly, 'There's one way to find out,' nodding to the stethoscope hanging around the doctor's neck, it was identical to his own.

The doctor put his stethoscope to his ears and listened first to Sam's back and then to his front. 'It's probably nothing to worry about but there is a faint murmur old son. May have to jump start you one of these days. I know it sounds like teaching your grandmother to suck eggs, but if you begin to feel unusually fatigued or notice any quickening in your heart rate, well you know the drill. Now what else can I do for you? Sam handed him the car licence form. He then endured a variety of basic cognitive and co-ordinance tests, such as putting his finger on his nose with his eyes shut, and standing on one leg. His peripheral vision, the doctor claimed was better than average for his age and probably better than his own. His cognitive responses were passable, just, as was his coordination.

'Where's that jolly form? There you are, you are mobile for another three years,' the doctor said, scribbling an eligible signature. 'You will be at the mercy of some other poor bugger next time I'm afraid. I'll be off sailing and doing a spot of fishing in Hawks Bay this time next month and I will not be coming back, like you, a man of leisure. Best of luck Sam, take it easy.'

There was a message on his cell from Lois asking him if he would like to go with her to see the latest James Bond movie. They could grab an Indian meal afterwards. He answered yes, and suggested he pick her up. He congratulated himself on still having the use of his car. She called him again a day before they were due to go, to confirm the date which she had apparently forgotten. Sam had grown accustomed to her forgetfulness, it had seemed charming at first but over time he began to expect what he considered to be a form of idiosyncratic behaviour and he would find himself prompting her, putting a name to friends and dates sotto voce, when she was obviously struggling to remember. But then he could forgive her anything. It was an afterthought when he suggested they invite Dennis. The three had not been out together it seemed for ages. 'He has been very quiet lately. He cancelled our weekly chess game for some vague reason two weeks ago. You don't think his nose is out of joint?

'Why should it be?'

'Well I would have thought it obvious. He probably hates playing gooseberry.

'I'm sure there's no risk of that. Surely you know. Oh Gussie!' she exclaimed. 'Really, you can't be serious. '

'I have no idea, what you mean.' Sam replied, bewildered on two counts-genuinely having no idea what she was on about and wondering who the hell was Gussie?

'Darling you are sometimes so naive.'

'Am I missing something here?'

Lois burst into uncontrollable giggles.

'What for goodness sake?'

'Sweetheart you must have realised? Dennis is gay.'

Sam looked at her aghast. 'I really had no idea. You must think me an absolute idiot?'

'Welcome to the real world Darling. Why would you know or care? He's still our lovely entertaining Dennis isn't he? He hides his sexual proclivity well, something he probably does out of habit, it's the result of his living through a time of vile persecution for gay men. They threw people like Dennis into prison not too long ago if you recall. Poor Dennis has lived in fear for most of his life, imagine how dreadful it would be to suffer not just ridicule but hatred? He still lives a lie because it feels safer to pretend. All this reminiscing about his past experiences and associations is a kind of smoke screen.'

In fact, as Sam was to learn when he finally reached Dennis on his cell, he would have loved to have accompanied them to the Cinema. But as it happened Dennis was indisposed and was actually speaking from a hospital bed. Sam expressed concern but was assured it was only a matter of a few routine tests and a scan of some kind and so nothing about which to be alarmed. He would be back at the village later in the day. He declined Sam's offer of a lift home from the hospital and promised to continue their chess evenings.

When Sam saw him next, a few days later, Dennis was definitely not his ebullient self. He had lost weight and had a distinct yellow pallor. Sam knew Dennis was jaundiced and said so. He did not express his concern.

'Don't get putting on your medical hat old son. I've had this before. It's my misspent youth catching up with me. I've been punishing the old liver a little more than usual lately, nothing to worry about. It's time I gave up the grog completely, simply can't handle it like I used to.'

Sam was not convinced but said nothing. They played a desultory game of chess, neither had their hearts in it. Sam won easily. 'What did the hospital have to say?

'More tests. Wait and see. None of us are getting any younger are we? Never expected to make it this far. Just wish I didn't feel so damned tired all the time. I can drop off sometimes without knowing it. Let's not talk about it. So how are you and the lovely Lois getting on? Sam confessed it was sometimes hard for him to keep up with her. He changed the subject to the latest James Bond movie and how it might be Daniel Craig's final performance in the role.

'I knew Cubby Broccoli in the early days you know.' said Dennis, suddenly brightening up. 'He was an engaging character, more so than Harry Saltzman. I met them after they co-founded Eon and produced Doctor No out at Pinewood. I was just a dog's body, a Kiwi opportunist in a production assistant role. I was there at the very beginning, amazing really. A Yank and a Canadian in London with the film rights to the greatest film franchise ever in their pockets. Of course they both knew they were onto a winner but I doubt either of them realised then just how big it would become. Harry soon dipped out for one reason or another. I could never understand why. Then it became Cubby's show, in fact his whole life. He was tough but a charmer. He rarely failed to get his own way. Forty movies I think was the total. You know what, I could put together a James Bond season for the film society. Why don't we get all the early ones, show one a week and I can say a few words before and at the end to the group? Could take up to a year to wade through the lot.'

Sam agreed it would be a winner and felt sure it would go down well. But he looked at Dennis and hoped he would be up to it. As Dennis was leaving, claiming an early night was probably in order,

But a few weeks later Dennis was back in hospital for another series of scans. An ultrasound and an MRI scan were quickly followed by a CT scan. He texted Sam from the hospital and asked him to collect a few toiletries from his chalet because it seemed he would not be home for some time. 'I'll explain when you get here.' He said.

Sam let himself into Dennis's home, put together everything he had requested and packed them in a small travelling case. He added a couple of novels from his own bookshelf he thought he would enjoy. He checked everything was switched off. He drove to the hospital and found the ward where Dennis was lying on a cot with tubes hanging off him, connected to various monitoring devices. He sat next to him and unloaded what he had brought.

'So what's the diagnosis?' he asked, dreading the answer.

'Not so good Sam. The prognosis is pretty dodgy actually. Dennis smiled sadly. His face seemed sunken, his cheek bones prominent, there was a watery glazed stare in his eyes. I've had all the scans Sam and now it's certain. It's the end of the road I'm afraid. Tears welled up in his eyes he let them run down his face. Fucking pancreatic cancer Sam, stage four.' He whispered. Sam had suspected it but was still dismayed by the confirmation.

'Has it spread? Is there any sign of lymphoma?' Dennis nodded and bowed his head. Sam stood, leant forward and cradled Dennis's head in his arms.

They stayed like this until a senior nurse threw back the drapes and asked Sam to sit down. She checked the monitors, made a few notes and asked Dennis if he was comfortable. She tucked him into bed tightly, adjusted his pillows, looked at her watch and reminded Sam visiting hours had to be strictly observed.

When Sam left he stopped by reception, explained who he was and wondered if he could have a word with the senior person attending to Dennis. It would not have mattered if he had been Albert Schweitzer because no one was available to see him. He was not next of kin. In any event the privacy act restricted personal details being disclosed to anyone other than close family. He was reminded of visiting hours again and learnt nothing more.

He called Lois and told her the bad news. She seemed a little vague. Sam had to remind her of Dennis's previous hospital visit. Then she burst into tears, wailing, 'No, no. Not Dennis. Not Dennis, not Dennis.' He explained

 Brian Millard

how he intended to pull a few strings and find out more on his next visit the following day. He hung up to more sobbing. There was nothing he could say to console her. She asked if he would pick her up and they could go to the hospital together.

The word travelled fast through the retirement village like a whispered susurrus at first, then loudly and boldly. The merry widows had a field day. The following day at lunch Dennis was the main topic of conversation. One of the more socially aggressive of the ladies pigeonholed Sam and demanded to know the details and the visiting hours. He had no option but to tell her. He drove over to pick up Lois and in near silence drove slowly to the hospital. Lois seemed withdrawn and he was not sure what to say. It was not possible to make light of stage four Pancreatic Cancer, so he concentrated on his driving. It took time finding a park and when one became vacant it took him four attempts to park the Swift safely in the spot.

When they reached the public ward they found the merry widows congregated at Dennis's bedside, Sam was already feeling uncomfortably hot. There was no room for them to sit and no alternative but to wait outside of the ward. A child was misbehaving and the mother, a young, vacant looking woman, seemingly incapable of controlling the little girl, made the odd futile attempt to stop the child running about and making a noise but soon gave up. She sat sullenly and morosely facing Lois. They waited.

Finally the Merry Widows emerged from the ward still talking at the top of their voices. They caught sight of Sam and Lois in passing and ignored them. One said, '…was he delirious or what? What was all that rubbish about Joan Collins?'

'I think he was expecting a visit from her.' Another quipped cruelly.'

'Honestly, still full of it on his deathbed, spouting all that garbage about James Bond, unbelievable.'

'As I was saying to Cubby,' one of the other ladies added, which prompted all round laughter. The woman who had accosted Sam at lunch time was still grinning when she glanced at Lois and sniffed. They began to walk away.

Lois sprang to her feet and stood in their way. 'You obnoxious heartless bunch of bitches she said quietly. 'Dennis gave his everything to try to brighten your miserable little lives. He asked nothing from you. The very least you should do is show him a little respect.'

Sam stood, took her arm and they went into the ward leaving the Merry Widows looking decidedly not merry. When one went to speak, Sam stopped and turned he put a finger to his lip and gave the woman a look of utter contempt. The ignorant women thought better of it and scurried off after her cohorts.

Dennis was lying with his eyes closed. Lois went to him and kissed him. She stroked his hair. Dennis smiled. 'Lois,' he said, 'are you trying to take advantage? And Sam. Thank goodness for good friends. The Merry Widows were here. Thank God I'll soon be shut of that dreadful coven of old crones.' This elicited a whimper from Lois. 'Now there's no need for that. I've come to terms with it. I've lived well, probably too well. I've had a lovely time. Oh, I think I've pinched that line from dear old John le Mesurier. Remember him, married to Hattie Jacques? He was such a joy, such a talent. On his death bed he said "It's all been so lovely." Says it all don't you think?' Hattie only made it until she was fifty eight.' Lois took his hand and held it to her lips.

'Oh my Darling Dennis,' she whispered.

Sam excused himself and went in search of someone in charge. He eventually spoke to the specialist on Dennis's case. He learnt that Dennis needed to be moved into palliative care in a few days. He explained there was a problem with next of kin. Apparently there was none. There was a need for someone close to Dennis to have power of attorney and act on his behalf. This would determine where Dennis would go for the remainder of his life. He wondered if Sam was prepared to take on the role. If so, he would have to make a visit to Dennis's solicitor without delay. Sam went back to the ward and asked Dennis what he thought. Dennis nodded and gave him the name of his solicitor. Sam promised to report back after the meeting. 'It was,' he said 'the least he could do in the circumstances.' This prompted more kisses and tears from Lois whilst Sam, trying to remain as stoic as he could, attempted to hug his friend without dislodging any of the many tubes hanging from him. They left the hospital and Lois was returned to her apartment.

So Sam became the sole executer of Dennis's will and took on the duties and responsibilities inherent in having power of attorney. The solicitor pressed upon him to locate a suitable hospice or end of life organisation into which Dennis could be transferred within a few days. With the help of the retirement village nurse a suitable place was located. It was a newly build rest home offering the services to help terminally ill patients. It was, Sam thought, a soulless place, and rather austere. Although obviously clean and light, it was impersonal. At more than a thousand dollars a day, it promised individual care for each patient. It was 'family inclusive' whatever that meant. It promised compassion and respect, with expert hospice nurses on hand to give relief for those with 'life limiting' illnesses. A specialised 'end of life' care option was available. A free tour was also available. However, due to the short notice, a single room was not immediately available, and initially Dennis would be required to share a larger room with two other patients before being moved to a private room. Sam explained all this to Dennis and he smiled his thanks. He had been given morphine and it was kicking in. He was moved into care before the end of the week.

When Sam came to see him he found him in a large room containing two others beds curtained off to give a semblance of privacy. Dennis lay motionless on his bed, he was wearing plug-in ear phones and was listening to music on his laptop. Sam picked up the book Dennis had been reading and read a few lines then turned it over to the back cover. It was by a brilliant writer in the spy genre called John Layton. The very first paragraph grabbed him and he decided he would purchase another copy for his own bookshelf.

'Is that you Sam?' Dennis croaked faintly. He opened one eye. 'I thought as much. I was just listening to Ella. I've always been in love with her voice, it is so beautiful, immaculate timing, absolutely divine. Have you nothing better to do than visit inmates in the stalag?'

'I'll bugger off again if you like,' said Sam.

'No stick around, I'll introduce you to Eva Braun, she'll like you.'

'Dennis, it's far from a stalag. It's actually better than most places of its kind and certainly an improvement on a public hospital ward. You will be in a room of your own anyway in a couple of days. So stop complaining. It was the best I could do at short notice.'

'Sorry, it's because I'm dying. It's not as easy as I thought to come to terms with..'

Sam lifted one of Dennis's limp and lifeless hands and held it between his own, trying to pump some of his own life force into it.

'See that bloke in the corner?' Dennis indicated with a slight lift of his chin.

Sam peered at a figure curled up in a bed at the far end of the room. The man appeared to be comatose.

'Do you mean the one who's asleep?'

'Yes, he's very quiet, never speaks because he sleeps a lot. I mean all the time. He's practising if you ask me.'

'Practising for what?'

'For the big one, the big sleep'. This drew a reluctant, if rueful smile from Sam.

'Can you smell it?'

'Smell what?'

'Take a big sniff Sam, deep as you can see if you can identify it.'

Sam did as instructed.

'Well?'

'Well I'm getting a distinct pong of disinfectant overlaid by a rather musky hint of…well more than a hint actually, of ripe bedpan.'

'Close old son, not bad at all. It takes a couple of days to get the nose attuned. There's a base note in there of something else too, it reveals itself eventually, makes itself known particularly in the wee small hours.'

       Brian Millard

'I hate to ask what it is.'

'It's the smell of putrefaction Sam, the smell of death.'

Sam was lost for words. He was saved from more of the same desperate gallows humour by an overweight but very pleasant, even pretty young woman pushing a laden tea trolley.

'Sam, this is Eva, you will have to behave yourself now. Not for me Eva, I have very little appetite these days.' Sam dug in to the sandwiches.

When the nurse had gone Dennis had a request. He asked that, when the time came, Sam place death notices in The New Zealand Herald, The New York Times and The UK Daily Telegraph, and also in a selection of entertainment media that carried obituaries and death notices. Sam promised to make sure his wishes were carried out. There were other bequests, which he also agreed to follow explicitly. When Sam was about to leave Dennis clasped Sam's arm with surprising strength.

'Thanks old Son…Thanks for everything.'

The rest home was as good as its word and Dennis was moved into a comfortable, light filled room overlooking the grounds. There were mature trees, lawns and the sound of birds singing outside. He had his own television set and a little book case. He was there for three days and nights before he died. Sam was left to arrange his funeral and cremation. He enlisted the aid of the remaining two members of the bowling team. They were not much help. There was an embarrassing incident in Dennis's unit at the retirement village when one of the Merry Widows had the gall to volunteer her services and began to go through Dennis's personal stuff. Sam was forthright, even rude, and gave her short shrift. 'Madam you have no business here. Please leave now and close the door behind you!' He was as polite as his rising anger allowed.

'There's no need for that kind of talk, I was trying to do a good …'

Then Sam lost it. 'Are you deaf woman? Bugger off and don't come back! The woman gaped in amazement at the sudden transformation and scurried off muttering under her breath and slammed the door. Sam felt a fluttering in his chest and sat down for a few moments before returning to the job in hand.

Fortunately the retirement village had procedures in place to deal with a sudden death in the resident community when no family could be located. The young nurse from the medical centre was on hand to do most of the telephoning and email work in the organising of the funeral arrangements. This she did methodically and efficiently. It left Sam free to sort through Dennis's effects and make lists and record the items on his cell. Dennis had not been a hoarder but had definitely been reluctant to discard any memorabilia relating to his years in film and TV. He had kept endless press cutting and magazine articles, all filed neatly by year and date plus old videos and reels of film.

There was also an envelope with 'Sam' written on it in Dennis's cursive script. Inside there was a note to him and a small memory stick taped to it. The note read:

Dear Sam,

If you are reading this it means I have hung up my clogs sooner than you. You are probably trying to come to grips with your role of executor. In which case I wonder if you would kindly do me yet another kindness? You will find in this envelope a USB flash drive. On it I have compiled what I hope is an entertaining few minutes that encapsulates my life. I have enjoyed almost every second of living it and I would like to share it. It might also liven up the business of cremation a little. I would like it played on a big monitor at the funeral, I believe all the electronics are available at the crematorium. Use my laptop if you need to, I have left instructions on how to make it work. Any trouble, enlist the help of Nurse Debbie from the medical centre, she is invaluable. Please donate my books to the village library, take whatever you like of my paintings and other stuff, and give away the rest. My solicitor has my will, there isn't very much

 Brian Millard

by way of actual cash but what there is I feel sure you will see goes to where I have specified.

Whilst I still can I would like to say something to you on a more personal note: (Now don't get embarrassed). I need to tell you that it has been a real joy knowing you. Thank you for your support, your friendship and wise council. Thank you for everything.

See you soon old son.

With great affection
Dennis.

The funeral took place a couple of weeks later. It had been arranged that Sam would pick up Lois from the reception area of her retirement village as normal. He had never been invited up to her actual apartment. He had expected to wait a few minutes, but when, after twenty minutes, there was still no sign of Lois, he called her and asked her politely if she was ready. 'Ready?' There was a pause then a light laugh. Oh yes of course. Just give me a few more minutes Darling.' When she appeared some time later she was dressed in a fitted black twin set which flared at the waist. She also wore what was once called a fascinator, a small black hat with a veil which covered most of her face. It was a rather old fashioned get-up, but, Sam reasoned, probably all she had to fit the occasion. The buttons of her jacket had been done up incorrectly and Sam corrected this for her. Perhaps she had been apprehensive and out of sorts with the awful finality of the cremation and at the last moment had panicked about what was suitable attire because she had also chosen to wear wildly inappropriate florescent pink Nike trainers. Inured now to her inexplicable and bizarre behaviour Sam made no comment, another delay would make them late for the funeral where his presence was essential. He was expected to meet and greet the mourners and act as master of ceremonies. He helped her into his newly polished car and drove anxiously and over cautiously to the cemetery.

Lois sat in the front row, in a reserved seat close to a small podium, whilst Sam took his place at the door, greeting and ushering members of the congregation to seats as they arrived. Each received a leaflet with a photograph of Dennis grinning on its cover. In the reproduction Dennis's teeth looked extraordinary white and his face glowed with what could be easily mistaken as an artificial tan but was probably due to the quality of the printing. It was otherwise a respectable document prepared by the funeral company, containing a few lines by way of biography and spelling out the order of the speeches and so forth. Most of the retirement village turned up, including others from other retirement establishments who had known Dennis. When the merry widows arrived they ignored Sam. One grabbed a handful of leaflets. When they saw Lois sitting, head down in the front row, they argued amongst themselves quite loudly then started moving the reserved seat signs. Sam strode down the aisle and prevented them sitting in the reserved seats near her. One look at his face and his body language and they sidled off to another row near the front, making other guests shift along the row to make room for them. Sam sat next to Lois and held her hand. He was on his feet shortly afterwards when the hearse arrived. As Dennis had requested the coffin was a simple affair constructed of plywood. It was draped with a New Zealand flag and there were a few wreaths and bunches of flowers on top. The funeral director gave instructions to the pall bearers, and, with almost military precision, they removed the coffin from the hearse and took their places at either side of it. Sam and a few younger men acted as pall bearers. It was a relief to him to discover the burly funeral guys surrounding him had somehow conspired to take most of the weight. They carried the coffin slowly and carefully into the chapel and placed it on a gurney beside the podium.

The funeral director turned to Sam, bowed discretely and murmured 'Over to you.'

Sam moved to the podium. He had written a few notes but found he had no need of them. He spoke about the impact Dennis had had on

Brian Millard

the retirement village from the moment he arrived and how his presence enlivened the routine of the place, how he gave the residents something different to look forward to and enjoy. How he took over the running of the bowling team and organised competitions and tournaments and away games. What a good skipper he was, always encouraging and always able to devise strategies and game plans. How gracious he was in defeat and how generous with praise he was when the team won. He talked of his good humour, his easy manner and how he threw his energies into a myriad of projects without reward. He spoke of the film Society, the chess club and the quiz nights he created.

'Dennis was a one-off,' he said, looking around the room. He had had an extremely interesting life, and, to a large extent, what he achieved was done for the fun of it. It was his optimism and sense of fun that fuelled his adventures firstly in the film business and then in television in Britain. On the way he met many of the great personalities of the day. It was inevitable that his good looks and charm would attract similarly talented individuals. He made friends easily. People were drawn to him because he made them feel good about themselves and what they were doing. He was, in my humble opinion, like a ray of light in a place that can sometimes seem dull and, let's face it, even miserable. I can feel him saying, "Shut up Sam, you're embarrassing me."' Sam turned and addressed the coffin. 'Sorry Dennis your turn will come in a few minutes.'

He stood down and went back to his seat next to Lois, she held his hand, touched his cheek with her gloved hand. The funeral director introduced Debbie the village nurse. She praised Dennis, not just for his love of life but also for his tolerance and compassion. She gave a few instances and hinted that there were those who may have been jealous of him.

Members of the bowling team took the podium. 'He was a great bloke, one of the best. He was already missed.' There were a few other short, ill-prepared speeches. The funeral director stood and looking around him asked if anyone else wished to express their feelings about Dennis. One of the Merry Widows made an attempt to get up but was wisely retrained by her cohorts. The funeral director looked at Sam who took control of the microphone. Debbie took her place by a laptop.

'Well, I promised Dennis he would get his chance to address you all. He must have prepared what you are about to see now when he first realised the seriousness of his illness. Thank you Debbie,' said Sam. The lights dimmed and the strains of 'Gonna take a Sentimental Journey' sung by Ella Fitzgerald filled the chapel.

A photograph of Dennis as a little boy aged probably about three appeared on the screen and morphed into a schoolboy wearing the Kings College uniform. Already you could see the smile and the charm of the man. Then, in a group shot of Dennis in his early twenties on the deck of a large boat, he appears wearing a steward's uniform and is in the centre of half a dozen other young larrikins similarly dressed, behind them is a broad expanse of angry sea. Then an obviously posed professional portrait shot of Dennis grinning winningly at the camera.

This was following by a series of full length shots of Dennis wearing an assortment of formal and casual clothes. No doubt all part of a portfolio to be used by an agent.

Close ups of early film posters in which Dennis's name shared the billing with a variety of well-known British stars of the late forties and early fifties.

The music faded, to be replaced by a short movie of Dennis and Stewart Granger fencing with foils, both dressed in identical costume – they are so alike physically, it is difficult to tell who is who. The film ends with each of the duelists apparently receiving mortal wounds as they both stagger about exaggeratedly and finally fall, one on top of the other, then Dennis, unable to contain himself, apes Stan Laurel, gives a silly grin and ruffles his hair with a cupped hand. Stewart Granger sits up and pushes him off. This was a short clip from 'Scaramouche', which starred Janet Leigh and Mel Ferrer.

Then another snippet of film composed of out-takes from a film. Dennis is seen being repeatedly thrown down a flight of stairs. Each time he climbs back up the stairs it is only to be thrown down the stairs again by Alastair Sim. This footage is used to intersperse images from films as a sort of running joke. In the next sequence Dennis is seen from the back, kissing a dark haired girl passionately. She is bent over backwards in his arms. It is a long kiss, Dennis comes up for breathe turns his head to the camera pretends to wipe sweat from his brow gives a lecherous grin as he is pulled back down by a strikingly attractive young Margaret Lockwood for more of the same. Being a stand-in for Stewart Granger must have been tough, thought Sam.

More of the same followed from 'Young Bess'. Out-takes show Charles Lawton and Dennis in doublet and hose fooling about, in hysterics over something, with Jean Symonds and Deborah Kerr looking on, trying to stay aloof but also breaking up into laughter. Then a series of stills, fading one into the other appeared to more of Ella Fitzgerald singing 'Gonna take a sentimental Journey.' These shots were candid and showed Dennis mainly behind the camera or acting as focus puller for directors like Korda and Carol Reed. He is also shown in a variety of continuity roles, working at a desk with a mass of scripts piled around him, feet on the desk and a big sloppy grin on his face. Stills of him posing with Alec Guinness, John Mills, James Mason, Richard Attenborough, Patricia Roc, Mai Zetterling, Joan Collins, Deborah Kerr and many other personalities of the day, all morphed one into the next to the wonderful voice and perfect diction of Ella Fitzgerald .

This section of the video came to an end with a shot of Dennis standing between Cubby Brocoli and Harry Saltzman with their arms around each other's shoulders. The music continued as of the exterior of the BBC building and the Eric Gill relief carving featured above the entrance appeared, followed by an early black and white film clip of 'Dixon of Dock Green' showing Jack Warner saying something to camera, saluting and accidentally knocking his police helmet askew. Dennis appears from the side of the screen and adjusts it. He can't help playing to the camera and clearly mouths 'Evenin' all.' Other footage from a variety of British TV shows of the fifties, sixties and early seventies show Dennis working as a director, a producer and then a script editor. Patrick McGoohan is seen in 'The Prisoner' running along Portmeirion Beach, chased by a huge white ball. There are sequences and off-cuts from 'Upstairs, Downstairs', 'The Sweeney', 'John Thaw', 'Tinker Tailor Soldier Spy', Alec Guinness making another appearance, somewhat changed from his earlier one in the video when he was twenty years younger. Then a group shot of the entire cast and crew of the TV production of 'A Picture of Katherine Mansfield', starring Vanessa Redgrave, Dennis stands next to her in the centre. The sequence ends with a party. Film and television personalities are congregated in a swish restaurant, toasting a slightly overwhelmed looking Dennis. It is his farewell party and he is leaving Britain for New Zealand. A banner reads 'He's all yours-NZ God help you'.

In the last image, Dennis is seen shortly after coming to live at the Sunnyside retirement village. The shot had been captured by Lois on her cell phone at a bowling tournament. Dennis has his linen jacket over his shoulders and is leaning forward, he has been studying the state of play and she has caught him as he had lifted his eyes, recognised her and smiled. The image of his face was held on the screen until the music came to an end, then it faded.

Lois made it through the aftermath until the coffin was back in the hearse, she and Sam followed it for a few steps before Lois broke down and wept her heart out on Sam's shoulder. The rest of the group had descended on the catered lunch, the Merry Widows elbowing their way to the ham sandwiches, sausage rolls, chocolate éclairs and the white wine. Lois needing air went outside. Sam found her standing in a puddle in her pink Nikes, her veil askew and tears streaming down her face. The rain increased in severity, a severe downpour began in earnest. He pulled her into cover and hurried to his car, drove it to where she stood and took her home. No words were exchanged until they were in the foyer of her block of apartments.

He was about to depart when she took his hand and shaking her head wildly from side to side whispered, 'No, no you mustn't leave me.'

 Brian Millard

Her apartment was in complete disarray, clothing strewn everywhere, makeup and dirty dishes intermingling with half empty takeaway food containers. She disappeared into a bedroom and closed the door. Not sure what to do, Sam went to an armchair covered with newspapers and magazines and began to shift them in order to sit down but could not find a clear space on any surface to put them. He placed them tidily on the carpet amongst other debris. Then he heard music. He looked up and discovered Lois leaning back against the bedroom door dressed in an ankle length white wrap around dress. She had removed her make- up. The glitter, the false eyelashes gone. Her eyes seemed dull and grey. Had she worn coloured contact lenses, he wondered? Her youthfulness had now vanished. In repose her face and throat, devoid of artifice, betrayed her age. She appeared weary and desperately unhappy, yet her head was held high. In her hand she held a remote control of some kind, her eyes glazed, looking more inward than out. The remote dropped to the carpet.

The powerful voice of Jennifer Rush singing her anthem to the glory of sex, 'The Power of Love', filled the room. Sam listened and watched as Lois began slowly, almost imperceptivity at first, to move to the pounding, insistent beat of the music.

'*The whispers in the morning*
Of lovers sleeping tight
Are rolling by like thunder now
As I look into your eyes
I hold on to your whole body
And feel each move you make
Your voice is warm and tender
A love that I could not forsake…'

Then, her arms stretched into the air, the flaps of wrinkled skin hanging, no longer disguised, her back arched as she pushed herself from the wall and moved to match the percussion, her movements fluid and graceful. Sam gazed in wonder as she glided across the room. With her arms above her head she swayed, moving her head from side to side as if in torment. Sam watched transfixed as the music rose and swelled and she abandoned herself to it completely, her moves becoming increasingly more passionate and violent, her hair shaking loose and then, as if surrendering, falling to her knees and lying in the foetal position like a child.

She rose to her knees, reaching out imploringly, writhing on the carpet. Not once did she look at Sam, it was as if he was not there.

…'Cause I'm your lady
And you are my man
Whenever you reach for me
I'll do all that I can…

The music grew to a crescendo, the singer's voice soaring. Lois rose to her feet and began to pirouette on the balls of her feet, her arms wide. She threw herself down yet again and as the music swelled she moved in unison, jerking her arms and elbows violently and aggressively.

…Sometimes I am frightened
But I'm ready to learn
Of the power of love
The power of love

Lois, now spent, fell back again dramatically and, like a dying swan, fluttering, her arms outstretched, her face hidden, lay still. 'Oh Gussy darling, Gussy my love,' she whimpered, lifting her head, tears flowing down her face.

There it was again, thought Sam, 'Gussy'. Was this her new name for him? Sam felt an overwhelming sense of pity. She seemed so utterly fragile and vulnerable. He thought he must go to her in the hope of offering some kind of comfort. He stood and took the few steps to where she lay and looked down at the forlorn figure curled at his feet. He coughed politely and said, 'Lois, I think it's time I went home.'

Lois's eyes shot open. And she stared at him in absolute horror. She recoiled from him in fear, paddling backwards on her bottom, and screamed. 'Get away from me! Don't touch me. What are you doing?' Sam stood there stupidly, like a voyeur caught red handed. She screamed 'Who are you?' cowering from him. Sam took a step back and Lois scrambled to her feet, her arms flailing wildly- a hand caught him a stinging blow across the mouth. He tasted blood. She darted to a side table and picked up a table lamp, she looked ready to throw it.

Sam departed the scene hurriedly, his mouth smarting and bleeding. He tidied himself up as best he could in the corridor, fearful someone would come across him and wondering what excuse he could find if challenged. He let out his breath when he found the elevator empty and rode it down to the entrance. He sat in his car trying to pull himself together before the drive home. His medical training told him that Lois was seriously in need of neurological help. And who the hell was Gussy?

This question was answered during the following week, when the wife of a couple he had met at one of the bowls tournaments called to congratulate him on doing Dennis proud at the funeral. She and her husband lived in the same complex as Lois and on the same floor. It was a relief to hear that the woman only wished to say that she thought he had seen Dennis off with style. For one horrible moment he had thought her call was related to his hasty departure from Lois's apartment, but she had called simply to say how Trevor, her husband, had particularly enjoyed the video tribute to him. What a wonderfully full life Dennis had led. They had no idea he had been involved with the film industry to such an extent. She asked if Sam had realised that there was a beautiful wreath on the coffin with a handwritten message attached to it? He remembered a large bunch of flowers that looked expensive but had not had the opportunity to read the card. Apparently she had called her husband over to see it too. 'Well, it said something like- 'Here's to the good times Dennis Darling. And can you imagine, there was a lipstick imprint of a kiss on it.' She giggled. You would never guess who it was from.'

'So, who was it from?'

'Well it was it was from someone called Joan.'

'Joan? Joan who?'

'Joan Collins that's who, you know the film star, the sexy one. Bit of a dark horse our Dennis if you ask me? By the way, Lois is taking the loss of Dennis very hard, probably just one loss too many I expect. I don't wish to pry but how are *you* coping?'

'Coping in what way?'

'With her condition, her mood swings and all that.'

'Oh yes, sorry. Well coping is a good word, I am coping I suppose.'

'We have known Lois for years, knew her sister Margery. Lois was devastated when she died you know. When she lost her husband she invested her hopes of another life in Margery. She bought her apartment on our advice. We could sense what was happening to her but, well, she was an actress, after all, wasn't she, and good at hiding her emotions. It might have been different if she had been able to have children, but her husband was much older than she was, and the poor man was impotent. It didn't seem to matter, she loved him and he doted on her. It was a match made in heaven. The meds she's on don't seem to do much, they just make her dozy. The medical team at our village are in touch with her family in Scotland- seems it's pretty certain she will have to go into care.' Sam gasped. 'Didn't you know?'

'Actually I wasn't sure.'

'There's no cure for dementia is there? She nearly burnt the whole apartment block down the other week, forgot her iron was on, went to bed without a care in the world, the place was ready to burst into flames, smoke billowing out of the widows and alarms going off. One of the night staff got in with a spare key and put it out with an extinguisher. Poor woman lost it completely. Got out of bed with no clothes on and ran around screaming.

And she blew up a microwave, tried to nuke a can of beetroot. There was a massive explosion. It looked like blood splattered everywhere. She played music very loudly, drove everyone bonkers, sometimes the same tune over and over. No thought of the other residents. She left the water running in the bath. It went through the ceiling of the apartment below. It's been one disaster after the other these last few months. It's surprising you didn't know.'

'She didn't tell me.' Incidentally do you know who Gus or Gussie is? She has mentioned the name a few times.'

'Oh, that's her pet name for her late husband, Angus. He's been dead now for years. Scottish, of course, probably the only man she ever had a real relationship with actually, even though he was not much good in that department, you know, couldn't rise to the occasion, so there was nothing there for her. Who knows though, where there's a will there's a way. She would do anything for him, anything at all. He was a Laird or chief or whatever, you know, head of the clan, owned a stately home in the Highlands, would you believe?'

'I am so grateful to you. You have filled in a lot blanks for me and cleared up a bit of a mystery too. Thank you for telling me of the flowers and the card from Joan Collins as well. I know a few ladies who will be very interested to hear about that. I am so glad you got into touch. We will probably get together at the next bowls tournament.' He shut down his cell and breathed a sigh of relief, the guilt and some of the shame he had felt lifted from his shoulders, his own conclusions as to Lois's mental health confirmed. He had to accept their time together for what it was, part dream and part wishful thinking. Sam would never see Lois again but he often thought of her and the times they had enjoyed when he believed there had been a genuine tenderness and feeling between them.

By the time Sam was ninety years old, he had lost his driving licence and so became completely dependent on the village coach trips for outings and a change of scene. Cataracts threatened his eyesight and his legs could no longer be relied on to bear his weight. He used a walker more often than not. Occasionally an acquaintance would take him out of the village for a cheap meal or a coffee but mostly he found it more convenient to eat at the restaurant in the village. The meals were adequate but rather boring and predictable, new catering staff had not made a great deal of improvement after a first flurry of good intentions. The new management had decided the cost of the up-keep of the manicured turf bowling green was too high. The contractor retired and on his departure the grass was removed and replaced by perfectly flat artificial grass, requiring very little, if any maintenance. The bowling team had also undergone considerable change. None of the original team now wished to be involved. The reason being that for a while the team had fallen under the control of one of the remaining Merry Widows whose lack of bowling skill did not stop her being officious and attempting to rule the roost. Sam resigned from the team during this period. The woman was finally ousted from control and a new team was formed by younger new comers. Sam had lost interest in most activities apart from chess and reading. But the new team was in need of a skilled number four player and had heard of his prowess. Almost on the eve of their first tournament, Sam was cajoled and flattered into coming out of hibernation to fill his old spot. It was a home match, it involved no travel and he decided not to use his walker but rely on his walking stick to get to the green, then sit there in the sun until he was needed to bowl.

It was not the best of matches for either side. The new team did not play well together, each player vying to star and achieving nothing in the process. It was going to be a close finish. When it came to the last end the apposing team had two bowls placed close to the jack, so well placed it seemed an impossible feat to reverse the situation. The time came for Sam to deliver the final decisive bowl. He leaned on his walking stick and took his time in studying the land and the positions of the bowls. The artificial surface he had found not to his liking. He made his decision, took a deep breath and sent his bowl on its way. It seemed to take an eternity before it nudged the bowl closest to the jack out of play and nestled into the space between the

 Brian Millard

other bowl and the jack, coming to rest perfectly, a whisker between each. There was a bust of clapping in approval. Sam had gone down on his knees, a searing pain running down his left arm. It seemed a massive weight was pressing down on his chest. He tried to breath but could not. He fell face-forward into the new Astroturf and felt nothing from then on.

The game was over. Sam's final bowl had won the day. The applause that had broken out spontaneously came to an abrupt end when it was realised what had also happened. Shocked players and onlookers gathered on the green around him helplessly. The nurse was alerted. She came at a run carrying a defibrillator, turned him onto his back and tried to resuscitate him by mouth to mouth. When it became obvious there was no hope of response by this means, she put the pads to his chest and sent three hundred and sixty joules of energy into him in the hope of restarting his heart, she was on her third attempt when an ambulance arrived. A medic examined him and said quietly, 'He's gone,' closing Sam's eyes.

From someone in the crowd of onlookers came the words, 'Bloody good way to go if you ask me.'

The
Hallelujah
Chorus

A year in the life of a 9-year-old boy is a long time. He thought the kid whose parents owned the greengrocer shop, who was all of twelve years old, seemed really old and adult. One of the reasons being the older boy had a bike he used for making green grocery deliveries. He also belonged to the Church Choir. The young boy had been to Sunday school at the same church a couple of times under duress but had not continued. He had subsequently joined The Band of Hope, a religious organisation whose mission was to stamp out the evils of drink. The boy's reason for joining though was more prosaic. He had joined simply to be invited to the Christmas party. It was a great party with lots of trifle and jelly. He considered taking the 'Pledge', much to his father's amusement.

A year or so later he found himself a member of the church choir and would ride there most Saturdays and every Sunday morning on the crossbar of the greengrocer kid's bike whilst he peddled. On Saturday the choir sang at weddings. This was a huge boost to the boy's finances as he would receive in payment, two shillings per wedding. Adding this to his earnings delivering news papers elevated him to a young fellow of substance.

He was required to wear a cassock, a surplice and a stiff pleated ruff around his neck. The choir always made an entrance after the wedding party was assembled. On cue, the organ would strike up, and he would walk solemnly down the aisle in step with similarly attired choristers, their heads bowed reverently. There were a few adults and a couple of older kids in the choir who could carry a tune but most of them just winged it. In fact, at his debut wedding, he just lip-synched. No one seemed to care as long as he looked the part. He was also required to attend services on Sundays. With his shock of blond hair, he looked angelic. Appearances are deceptive. As soon as a service had concluded and the vicar and the verger no longer present, the choir would revert to type, the group of boys enthusiastically taking turns in sliding down the aisle in their socks to see who could slide the furthest. Quite often they would end up in a heap in front of the altar; a bunch of irreverent tykes, pretending to be choirboys, hooting with fun and without a shred of religion between them.

A few years passed profitably and the numbers of weddings increased. From being a pure soprano the boy's voice began to change, without warning it might drop to a baritone for a few notes before rising uncontrollably up to a high pitched falsetto. So high and sharp, in fact, that, in one rehearsal, when the choir master walked around whilst they sang and listened to each voice individually, he stopped when he came to the boy and listened intently. He shook his head at what he heard and walked away muttering something about it being 'shrill enough to shatter glass.'

Handel's Messiah was to be performed in Latin at a cathedral nearby. Probably just to swell the ranks and to add a bit of window dressing, the fraudulent choir was roped in to sing at two performances. They dutifully turned up to the cathedral and took their places in the front of the massed choirs of the Midlands. There were singers of all ages and both sexes, in banks of tiered pews on both sides of the nave. The boys were given sheet music with their parts annotated, even though not one of them could read a note of music and quite a few could not read at all. The choirmaster stood poised directly in front of the boy. The organ started up and the massed choir burst into song.

He mimed convincingly for a while until he realised there was a repetitive chorus of hallelujahs. When the Hallelujah Chorus came around again he tentatively joined in. The strength of his voice grew louder as his confidence increased. Soon he was belting out 'Hallelujah! Hallelujah! Hallyeeloohuhhuyar!' with the rest of them and enjoying himself. He was at full throttle when his vocal chords rebelled and decided to go their own way, running through different levels of pitch uncontrollably. The conductor raised his eyebrows and cast about him frantically until he located the source of the offending voice and looked at the boy in alarm. For a few moments their eyes locked in mutual panic.

The boy learnt later that the performance had been recorded for broadcast on the Third Programme, but as his father could not abide listening to 'such tripe' he never heard it.

Guilt

His pocket money was erratic, negligible. It was supposed to be seven pence a week. A penny a year for each year he had been around. He believed he could look forward confidently to an increase of a penny on every birthday, it meant he would have the sum of one and six when he was eighteen.

It was the boy's mother's birthday, and he wanted to buy her a gift. He went to Woolworths in the hope of finding something for her he could afford. In those days the store displayed no end of merchandise on sloping display counters. Amongst them were displays of cheap jewellery. He spotted a pair of marquisette earrings in the shape of horseshoes. They cost possibly little more than a shilling but still more than he could afford. No one saw him slip the earrings into his pocket. He knew right from wrong and was aware he had stepped over a line. Yet he felt excited and petrified at the same time. A theft is a theft, and it might just well have been the Crown Jewels he had shoplifted. He should have known better. His mother was delighted with the earrings. She loved them and each time she wore them would say, 'See, I'm wearing my favourite earrings.' Each time she did, the boy felt worse about his crime, especially because he had led his mother to believe he had saved up to buy them.

Sometime later his mother lost one of the earrings. She was very upset and wept when she told him how sorry she was to have been so careless after he had saved his pocket money for so long to buy them for her. He wanted to tell her not to worry because he had not paid for them but had pinched them, but, as much as he wanted to, he could not bring himself to confess. His mother had a good idea where she may have lost the earring. She described the place, a grass verge not too far away. He went there after school and searched through every single blade of grass for hours until he saw the familiar shape of a tiny horse shoe glistening in the grass. His mother was overjoyed to be reunited with her precious earring and wept again, and the boy learnt an important lesson.

 Brian Millard

The games
we play

It was his weekend to have the twins. He had taken the girls to the cinema, eaten junk food. They had walked on the beach. It had been less strained than other similar weekends. They were larking about and feeling quite happy when he delivered them back to the family home. He had been surprised, well amazed when Jenny invited him to come over the next weekend 'to talk'. The children would be staying at a church camp.

Ralph turned up at the appointed time not knowing what to expect. He was feeling apprehensive when he knocked on his own front door. It had been only a year since he had thrown up his job on the Boston Globe and brought his family back home to New Zealand to a job as political correspondent on the Otago Daily Times. It had not taken long for the old issues to crop up. Reluctantly he had agreed to a brief separation and moved out.

Jenny seemed pleased to see him. It was the first time he had been allowed into the family home since leaving some eight months ago. It was pristine and smelt of Pledge furniture spray. The American furniture they had bought back from Boston looked like new. He sat in the overstuffed chesterfield couch which had seemed perfectly suited to their old Boston house but now seemed ostentatious and out of place. He sank into it. He was startled when Jenny stood before him her hands on her hips, loosened her hair, raised her skirt and straddled him. He was genuinely taken by surprise. It was something she had never done before and seemed such a clumsy attempt at seduction that he laughed. When he failed to respond, she pulled herself off his lap, straightened her skirt and said sweetly.

'Kevin had sex with me on their bed while Sue watched.'

By now he was almost in hysterics.

'You don't believe me do you?'

'No I don't,' he said.

He could not believe that she, the bloke next door and his wife could possibly have been involved in a threesome – they too, after all, were religious. He simply did not believe it.

'Tell you what,' he said, sarcastically. 'Let's go next door and ask Kevin and whatever her name is, if it's true?' Jenny picked up her cell phone and informed their neighbours they were coming over.

One glance at Kevin's sheepish and guilty expression was enough to convince Ralph of the veracity of what Jenny had told him. They followed him into the living room without a word being spoken. Susan, Kevin's wife, giving a very good impression of Debbie Reynolds, invited Ralph to sit down and primly asked if they would like tea or coffee.

'So is it true?' Ralph asked Kevin who hung his head 'I understand you've been having sex with my wife?' Kevin did not, could not, look him in the eye.

'Do you take sugar?' asked Susan.

'Well?'

'Yes it's true,' said Susan.

It was so incongruous and utterly out of character for Jenny to have behaved in such a fashion that Ralph still half believed it was some sort of sick joke.

'Well I hope you took your rollers out for the occasion?' He quipped to Jenny who was sipping her tea. She looked at him blankly. He was the only one grinning.

'Did you do it after a prayer meeting as a bit of light relief?' He threw in for good measure. They looked at him as if he had broken wind.

'Let's all go out', chirped Susan.

'Go out, where?' He asked, confused but curious.

'We know a nice little club', said Susan. She looked at Jenny, her neat eyebrows raised, nodding imperceptivity. Jenny was already on her feet. Kevin went to the bathroom. He came back wearing a jacket and tie.

Ralph watched his wife climb into Kevin's company car and sit in the front seat beside him. Debbie sat behind them. Ralph still stunned but intrigued, followed them in his own car. Kevin drove into Dunedin and parked near the Octagon. He did the same. He followed them into a side street and down an ally way, to an unmarked entrance. Kevin walked in, paid an entrance fee to a large Māori guy. They all entered. Kevin and Debbie parked themselves in the back row of a small theatre. Susan led Ralph by the arm and indicated he should sit with her, in the front row. The lights dimmed, Ralph expected to see some kind of burlesque show. He followed her along the row and sat as instructed, beside her.

A spotlight pierced the blackness on the stage. After a few minutes canned music struck up and stepping daintily into the circle of light appeared a male figure. He could have been Māori or Samoan. He was wearing a sparkling, sequined covered bra and a similar thong, cutting into his buttocks. The spotlight followed him as he strutted to and fro across the stage in very high heels. He swirled and posed, sticking out his bony backside in a parody of female provocation in time with the beat of the music. He first removed his bra, exposing a sunken chest and prominent ribs. More parading and posturing followed. With a flourish the thong was next to be removed. He stood preening before them stark naked. It was then obvious that he had no penis. He seemed proud of this and pointed at where one no doubt used to be. He put his hand to his mouth feigning shock. He glided over to a small table and lit a cigarette. He took a couple of puffs and strutted about a little more before crouching slightly and inserting the unlit end of the cigarette into a hole where once had been his male member. The music grew to a crescendo. The cigarette glowed brighter and then not so bright. This was repeated until smoke swirled around it. Smoke seemingly having been drawn in and then expelled.

Ralph stood up and said 'I've had enough of this,' and made for the exit.

Susan who had put on her glasses, was peering short sightedly at the stage. Realising Ralph was leaving she also stood up and followed him. As they passed the back row she whispered to the entwined figures of her husband and Jenny that 'he' wanted to go. Ralph walked briskly down the street to his car with the three of them following him. He was almost at his car when he heard a cry.

He turned and saw Jenny splayed on the footpath, her skirt up around her waist. One of her high heeled shoes was lacking a heel which was stuck in a crack in the footpath. She was obviously in pain. Kevin and Susan looked on uncertain what to do. Instinctively, Ralph ran back and knelt beside his wife.

'I've damaged my ankle,' she said 'Take me home, please.'

Ralph helped her up and half carried her, she clinging to him, hopping on one leg, back to his car, He drove off leaving the other two looking dazed. Nothing was said on the journey to the family home. He helped her out of the car and to the front door.

She looked at him and said, 'Well do you want to come in?' The kids are sleeping over at the church camp tonight.'

Ralph smiled sadly, shook his head, 'No thanks he said quietly.'

Bliss

The front door was locked. She found the key without any trouble at all. A pair of green wellies stood next to a pot of pink cyclamen on the York stone door step. The key was where you might expect, under the flower pot. A glance at the alarm panel she could see from the glass side window told her it was not switched on. Her reconnaissance had convinced her that the place was empty but there had been changes since her previous visit a couple of days earlier when she had explored the outer buildings. Then there had been a vintage red MG and a new Audi station wagon locked away safely in the garage. Today the garage was empty. The tool shed was now also locked when, before, it had been left open and had contained tools and a sit-on lawnmower, but it too was now empty. The outer buildings also were all securely locked. The stables were not locked but empty. There was not even a bale of hay to show they had ever been in use. One whole wing of the house, she determined by peering through the windows, was also totally empty of furnishings. The place could easily be used as a small hotel and was far too large for a regular family. Staff would certainly be needed to run it. Only one wing of this massive home appeared to be in use.

She slipped on her latex gloves and rang the door bell. She did not expect a response and there wasn't one. She opened the door, leaned in and just to be absolutely sure, sang out cheerily 'Hello, anyone home?' All was silent. She took off her shoes and walked confidently into the hallway.

If seen on the street or sitting in the lecture theatre at her university, it is more than possible Lisa Swan aged twenty three would go unnoticed, everything about her was average, she was of average height and build. She was attractive but in an average kind of way, nothing stood out. She dressed in an average manner and behaved in an average way. If anything she could appear somewhat diffident and rather quiet, she rarely expressed a point of view or argued with any force about anything. What friends she had found her reliable and pleasant but that was as far as it went. This in fact was exactly what Lisa wanted. She was a good daughter to her parents who considered her a late gift in the autumn of their years. Her father a jobbing builder who could turn his hand to anything in the building trade doted on her. He and his little girl spent a great deal of time together in his workshop. He, happy to share his knowledge and teach her skills normally passed on to a son, and Lisa, a willing and able student. Her parents were delighted when she gained entrance to the university but surprised by the subject she chose to major in and study. Anthropology was something they needed to Google in order to understand what it actually was.

Lisa liked to think that what she was doing could not remotely be termed burglary because she never stole anything. When the time came for her to deliver her dissertation and the final step in her PhD was in place, she was convinced what she considered to be a non invasive form of home invasion, would be justified. She was after all an anthropologist engaged on research 'in the field', albeit in homes belonging to people she did not know and illicitly. She was collecting data which could not be acquired in any other way. The very first time she had crept into a stranger's home she had been a bag of nerves and made countless mistakes. Taking that first step had not been easy but after many successful forays and as the data she collected grew, the more she was able to convince herself that the ends justified the means and it became easier. It even had a certain dare devil quality which she found exhilarating and left her feeling more alive. Her photographs and

 Brian Millard

notes were filed in a safe place ready for use in her dissertation. It would be the longest piece of writing she had ever produced. She already had the title: *Nonparametric statistics for the social sciences: Facts about real lives.* She believed her PhD was well in sight.

There was a pair of men's Sperry slip-ons size eight and a pair of lady's Jimmy Choo sandals size six on a shoe rack behind the door in the hall. She took a shot of their exact positions and placement on the rack and noted the details. This was her normal practice and in this manner she could build a profile of the subjects. The Jimmy Choo sandals fitted her perfectly. She decided to wear them for the time being and so put her own Doc Martens into her canvas shoulder bag. She could see the floors of the rooms off the hall had rich, deep carpet which would leave footprints. Any foreign impression would be obvious but the impression of the Jimmy Choo sandals would blend in and go unnoticed. As she wandered from room to room, any object that caught her interest was recorded on her cell phone.

In the kitchen she discovered the large double refrigerator was empty except for a few bottles of Bols champagne. She presumed perishables had been thrown out, again an indication the owners of the house expected to be away for some time. The walk- in pantry however was well stocked with canned and dry foodstuffs. She noted the brands and amounts, most of which were all top line and expensive, cans of truffles and Beluga caviar were neatly stacked next to an array of exotic condiments all of which carried the Fortnum and Mason emblem, Italian and Indonesian food apparently being the preference of the house owners. On a bench in the pantry were displayed an array of new matching mixers and blenders. Copper cooking implements hung above a granite work island. The cooking area was of contemporary German design, set against a rough brick wall. The cooking surfaces comprised of restrained greys and light coloured timbers. She noted that the oven tops and ovens showed little sign of use, if any. The waste disposal sink had no detectable odour, neither did the other sinks. A state of the art coffee maker sat on the granite kitchen bench top, she could smell coffee and found the remains of recent use. She looked inside the dishwasher and was not surprised to discover coffee cups and saucers waiting to be washed. The kitchen had been so thoroughly cleaned or so little used it was like a display setting in an upmarket store. This was interesting and certainly worthy of recording. It begged the question of how did the occupants normally eat and where? The dining area offered no clues, being just as sterile and soulless as the kitchen. She went into the sitting room and was relieved to find signs of occupancy. Someone had lounged in the large white couch. The cushions were scattered, one on the carpet, an indention in another. A coffee cup had been left on the coffee table, bright red lipstick staining the rim. She touched nothing, recorded everything on her cell. The design of the furniture was Spartan, low to the floor, simple lines, greys again, relieved by white cushions, pottery and ceramics also white with the occasional soft delft blue highlight. She noted the decor as the work of a professional interior designer. Large original art work in simple grey frames filled the walls, contemporary work, one composed of slabs of overlapping black gestural strokes. Another more formal, an abstracted landscape featured a large stark symbol of what may have been a cliff face with crudely rendered hints of perhaps trees leaning against the wind, broad horizontal strokes below, dribbles of dark blue and green, splatters of white paint that may or may not indicate sea.

A brilliantly colourful Mexican rug dominated the room. A couple of books lay on the coffee table, an empty plastic folder discarded on the rug. She recorded what she saw omitting nothing. She picked up the book, a thriller by Mo Hayder. She thumbed through it. Put it back exactly where it had been. Did the same with the other book 'Eat, Pray, Love' by Elizabeth Gordon. Titles more popular with female readers she noted, an image of the woman owner forming hazily in her mind.

Lisa went back into the hall, passing the staircase she noted a door set under the stairs with an old fashioned heavy ornate key in the lock. A room opposite the staircase contained a rumpled double bed that had seen recent use. A man's shirt lay crumpled beside it. On a hanger on a hook behind the door, a man's dark jacket and a pair of neatly pressed matching trousers, a striped, old school or regimental tie draped across a shoulder of the jacket. She went to the bed. Both sets of pillows were indented. She put her nose to one and detected male cologne, possibly Brut. On the other still lingered the unmistakable scent of 'Bliss', a perfume made famous by Angelino Jolie. Whoever this woman was she had expensive tastes and the man also had style. On one side table stood a half empty flute of champagne, red lipstick stains around the rim, another empty flute on the floor on the other side. She checked under the bed, opened the dressing table drawers found nothing, not even a fluff ball or a cobweb.

There was a bathroom and a dressing room off the bedroom, a double sink and a generous grey marble shower with enough space to hold a modest cocktail party, a separate claw foot bath. Above the bath a small window near the ceiling, on one side of the double sink an electric tooth brush and shaving gear, a few dark hairs caught in the shaver. On the other side, utter chaos. Beauty products scattered carelessly in the sink. A bra and pair of knickers tossed in a corner. From a hairbrush on the side of the bath trailed long blonde hairs. She picked up a bottle of Bliss Mon Guerlain, unscrewed the lid and breathed in its luscious, seductive scent. She knew it was wrong, possibly dangerous but she could not resist dabbing a liberal amount, first on the inside of her wrist and then behind her ears and between her cleavage. Somehow more of the perfume escaped the bottle than she intended and trickled down to into her bra and between her breasts. She turned on the tap in the sink and hopelessly tried to wash it off and, in the process, soaked her dress, which was now also reeking with Bliss. She took the dress off and stuffed it and her bra into her canvas bag.

She found being virtually naked in a stranger's home thrilling. Free of constraints and boundaries. As if she had taken on, by some kind of osmosis, the persona of someone else. Although surprised at the revelation, she welcomed the release from her normal self-imposed control.

She floated out of the bathroom in a cloud of perfume and through the door into the dressing room. It was lined with cupboards, shelves, and garment racks, hanging on them were dresses and gowns, jackets and slacks, suits and long overcoats from leading fashion houses around the world. None of the garments appeared to have been worn, some were still in their original coverings and carrying their original swinging shop labels. Another wall was lined with shelves of shoes by top designers, they were all her size, and the hanging garments would fit her perfectly, she wondered seriously if she dare try on something so expensive, took out a clinging evening dress. She stood before a full length cheval mirror, held it against her body and admired the way it clung to the curves she had forgotten she possessed. She put it carefully back on its hanger, the label told her it was a white flora rose silk, floor-length dress by Dolce and Gabbana.

She barely dared to examine the draws containing lingerie but could not resist, selected an exquisite lace bra by Coco de Mere and held it to her breasts. She appraised her image in the mirror, turning one way and the other. It was then she heard a car draw up on the gravel drive outside. She dropped the bra back into the draw and ran to the window of the bedroom. From a shiny black Lexus emerged a smartly dressed woman in her early thirties with beautiful long blonde hair, She went to the back of the vehicle, opened the rear door and bent over to extract something.

Suddenly remembering the sandals she was wearing, the near naked Lisa flew out of the room and along the hall to the front door, kicked them off and shoved them back approximating where they had been positioned before. She raced back down the hall, past the stairs and into the bedroom to the safety of the bathroom, leaving the door not quite closed. She listened intently and heard the front door opening. After a while, the sound of clattering crockery and running water came from the kitchen, a cell phone rang. The woman answered and said something quietly. Lisa could catch only a few words.

'Just a few minutes ago, thought you'd be here…' There was a brief pause before she heard a throaty laugh followed by, '… well I'm in the mood, it's celebration time isn't it.' Ten minutes passed before Lisa was startled

     Brian Millard

by the sound of a champagne cork being popped. She could not afford to be caught and considered making a run for it? She picked up her bag and carefully put her head around the bathroom door. She withdrew it sharply as the door to the bedroom opened. She panicked for a moment but then after taking a deep breath managed to compose herself. She decided to stuff her bag carefully and silently in behind the rack of designer dresses. Just as silently she slid behind a Victoria Beckham evening dress and a gorgeous Stella McCartney camel wrap-around overcoat with a wide collar and a long camel tie belt. She sat sidewards on her canvas bag knowing she was now in serious trouble.

So much for disciplined field work, she had broken one of her own cardinal rules. If only she had not taken that first step and touched the bottle of perfume. Stupidly, she had allowed herself to be seduced by the sensual scent of Bliss and the labels on the clothing. And as if that wasn't enough, she was also as good as naked. She almost fainted as the bathroom door was suddenly pushed open. She stifled a gasp and held her breath. To her horror she realised the woman was now in the bathroom, only a few metres away from where she was hiding and was using the toilet. She listened to her peeing and flushing, washing her hands. After what seemed an age, the woman went back into the bedroom. Lisa had no alternative but to stay where she was and although cramped and not too warm, she tried not to move or breathe. Should she sneeze or cough she would certainly be discovered.

There was no point in blaming herself for being stupid so she put her mind to ways the incident might be utilised in her research. Unprofessional or not, the situation could be seen in a positive light, and might be turned to her advantage. Let's face it she thought, no amount of canvassing would illicit this kind of intimate, closely observed information. Focus groups were all well and good but never produced such truly rare and valuable material, the participants are normally far too inhibited. She fumbled for her cell and wondered if it was possible to record the phone conversation from where she was, she could try. She could not see too well, smothered as she was in cashmere, and she almost dropped her cell phone, it bounced in her hand and landed in the pocket of the Stella McCartney overcoat. Where's your trade craft? She was admonishing herself silently when she heard the sound of another vehicle pulling up outside.

'Honey I'm home,' a male voice sang out. 'Where are you?'

'In the lust pad, I'm onto my second glass and waiting.' Through the gap in the door, the girl saw, for a fleeting moment, a male figure enter the bedroom and embrace the blonde woman, who handed him a flute of champagne. 'Had a profitable day?'

'Have you checked your bank balance? Your share went in an hour ago'.

'So we're finally in the money at long last?'

'Big Boris likes to play mind games. It's a power thing. Quite honesty I am almost clean out of charm and arse licking after eighteen months graft. The bugger kept me waiting most of the day, Thank God your work on Tatiana paid off again.'

'So did I get a big bonus?'

'Nobody got a bonus sorry. Anyway she had a quiet word with him and he made a call from another room, didn't say a word to me. She must have seen how I was feeling. She still didn't put me out of my misery until the last moment. I had started the car and was ready to drive off, wondering if I could give them a piece of my mind. Of course that would definitely have put the kybosh on the deal if I had. Anyway nice as you like, she puts her head in the car window and tells me finally that the money has gone off to Sir Barry and that we had been paid as well. She thanked us for all our good work, even pecked me on the cheek, the saucy bitch. So I called Sir Barry, he was at his holiday place in Jamaica, sounded like he had been on the piss and I gave him the good news. He didn't seem to care one way or the other. But apart from one or two loose ends it's a done deal. Could not have done it without you and that's for sure.'

The woman with the blonde hair reached for her cell and checked her bank balance. 'Oh Rod we pulled it off. That's one hell of a lot of money,'

     Brian Millard

she giggled. Lisa stared unbelievingly as the blond woman began to loosen the man's trousers which fell to the carpet. She gaped as he stood in his shirt tails. It was obvious where the disrobing would end. Lisa was transfixed, not knowing if she should look or not, she also wondered what on earth they were talking about. Whatever it was it sounded distinctly dodgy. The man was now down to his underpants.

'There was chance that Tatiana wouldn't get her way. She is determined to develop this pile into a horse stud, come hell or high water,' said the woman.'

'I'm sure Big Boris really couldn't give a damn one way or the other. He could buy Scotland, Wales and Ireland as well, if he felt like it.'

'She told me he is still best mates with Putin and the rest of his merry band of oligarchs. But you know I actually like her. She has style and certainly knows how to shop. She's just a very good looking young woman on the make, like we all are. In a way I feel sorry for her,' said the blonde. Lisa watched as she unzipped her skirt and stepped out of it. 'To the victor go the spoils.' They clicked glasses, threw back the champagne and fell onto the bed, 'Oh goody,' she whooped, 'would you look at that, a standing ovation and just for me.'

Unable to draw her eyes away, Lisa watched as the couple copulated, going at it with a vengeance. The blond woman now had her back to Lisa, and two smooth well formed buttocks rose and fell rhythmically.

There had been absolutely no foreplay and no words of endearment. It seemed to Lisa as if the performance she was witnessing was purely functional, simply a way of filling a basic human need and devoid of true tenderness and love. She tried to think of a few ways she could make use of such material in her dissertation. In her mind editing and redacting colloquialisms and crudity in an attempt to appear unbiased and clinical. She looked on fascinated. It seemed likely she was witnessing an adulterous and temporary relationship which could well be the norm for the demographic segment. But how to describe it in an acceptable manner for peer assessment was the problem. She searched for a way of describing what she was seeing in academic terms. She tried '*Involved in a tryst.*' and changed it to '*Engaged in sexual congress.*' She considered this not expressive enough so altered it to the less discreet but more academic, '*Observed 'in flagrante delicto'*'. The couple finally lay panting in each others' arms. Lisa considered making a dash for the bedroom door but when the blonde woman stirred, again changed her mind.

'Rod?' the blonde said. Do you think Jessica suspects?'

'Not a chance,'

'How about Jerry,' he countered, 'doesn't he wonder where *you* are now?'

'As long as I'm back in time to cook his dinner, well at least bung it into the micro wave before he gets home, he's as happy as a pig in the proverbial. Why do you ask? This is it the last time for a while. Any love stuff and you know it ends totally.'

'Just wondered, but I will miss you, you know.'

'I know exactly what you mean. Just imagine how much harm it would cause, think of Jessica and the children. Think of *my* position for God's sake. I would never hurt Jerry. It's been fun but it's time to go back to real life.'

'OK, message received, it's time. Look there's nothing to prevent you from getting back to Jerry and his pace-maker as soon as you like. I need to attend to a few loose ends here. The furniture goes back next week to the staging people and the place will need to be professionally cleaned. I can't walk away until that's done. The security company will be here later on that day as well. I'll need to be here to supervise the new security system installation and learn how it works. There's a chap coming to tidy up the garden, he'll need to be briefed. You don't need to be here until the week afterwards when Boris and Tatiana arrive for the key ceremony. I was hoping Sir Barry would also grace us with his presence but we will have to do without him. Now he's flush, he'll probably stay in the Caribbean and who can blame him? He is out of the scene on this particular project anyway. He's been a great client but will still need wooing. He has other property, so I will stay on his tail. Anyway what's the story with the designer gear in the changing room and the wine in the

 Brian Millard

cellar, any instructions from the princess? He stood up, stretched and stood hands on hips, looking, it seemed, directly at Lisa, who instinctively averted her eyes as he continued speaking. 'I feel sure Tatiana left all those expensive garments just to stake her claim. They stay, but will go upstairs to the master suite. Tatiana will be bringing a stack more of the same when they decide to move in. The wine in the cellar stays and a lot more will be delivered.'

'I'll race you to the shower,' said the blonde.

Lisa withdrew her head smartly and disappeared into the confines of the wardrobe. She listened as the guy came into the bathroom and released a torrent of urine into the toilet bowl, then flushed. The woman turned on the shower.

'Chrissie that perfume of yours is a little overpowering. Don't forget to take it home or it will get dumped, dirty knickers, everything, toiletries the lot.' Chrissie reached for a flannel from the towel rail behind him, a breast pushed into his face. 'Now look what you've done.'

'My goodness can't you control that thing?' she said. They both stumbled into the shower, and gasps of pleasure ensued once more. 'Oh my, slowly, slowly, yes there, just there, Oh my God. They don't call you *The Rod* for nothing do they?'

The unwitting voyeur shut her eyes and put her hands over her ears. After some time she realised the shower was no longer running and Chrissie and Rod were back in the bedroom. She could hear Chrissie. 'Got to hand it to you Rod the way you handled Big Boris was brilliant.'

'Babe I could not have done it without you. Seriously, I mean just look at the work you have put into Tatiana. You are like sisters.'

'All girls together, no problem, we speak the same language even if she is Russian. Girl power is universal, haven't you realised? I don't think for one minute I would get very far with Mr Big. I can't stand his bloody bodyguards. They scare me, big ugly thugs. Don't you feel just a little intimidated by them?'

'You want the truth? They bloody petrify me. That Dmitri's no more a chauffeur than I am and the other oaf who is supposed to be a man servant displays all the mannerisms of a psychopath, he's got the charm of a trained killer. He looks at me in a funny way and really puts the shits up me.'

'So what is Boris's real game do you think? OK, I can understand him pandering to Tatiana's whims and buying the place for her to play at being horsewoman of the year, but I sense there's a lot more going on.'

'It's pretty simple really, you buy a going concern with dirty money, then make improvements, and then flip it. Voila! Clean money comes out the other end. He's got interests like this all over the place, scores of businesses, doesn't matter if they make a profit or not. He must have stacks of other properties. So they turn this into a fancy horse stud, plough cash into it and then sell it. It's not exactly Rhodes Scholar stuff is it and perfectly legal. But honestly for me the project has gone on far too long and it's been extremely stressful. I'm sure Boris can't be trusted. You wouldn't want to offend him or cross him, believe me. He's completely unpredictable, I always feel uneasy around him and his bodyguards. I just can't read him. I haven't slept properly for a year or more.'

In some ways, Lisa wished she had not learnt their names, she had grown to like them, envied the uninhibited pleasure they took in each other's bodies and the light-hearted, matter-of-fact way they showed no regard for the immorality of what they were doing. She reminded herself that they were subjects under study and that she ran the risk of compromising her impartiality if she allowed her critical appraisal to lapse. She was sure she had stumbled onto a rich vein of material unlikely to be explored by others. Yet the more she learnt about the people they were involved with, the more fascinated she became, even if it all sounded like a farfetched movie on Netflix.

All she had to do was get away safely and start writing. It had grown quiet in the bedroom, she wondered if perhaps one or both of them had left the room. She pulled back the protection of the camel coat and tried to move. One leg had grown numb, went into spasm and she almost fell. She gasped out loud. For a few moments she stood frozen to the spot, but no one came to investigate. She rubbed her thigh back into life and listened for the faintest sound but all was silent. She came to the conclusion that they were in the kitchen. It was understandable that after all the energy spent by Rod and Chrissie over the last hour, a light lunch courtesy of Fortnum and Mason would certainly be in order. She was feeling hungry herself and also in need of the toilet, both would have to be put on hold until she was sure it was safe to move. So she stayed where she was. However the need to pee became urgent. She closed the bathroom door carefully and used the toilet as quietly as possible. She crept out into the bedroom, carrying her canvas bag, and tiptoed to the door, moved down the hall and stood flat against the wall beside the kitchen door, listening to the sound of crockery being placed into the dishwasher and more conversation.

'You may as well take your pick of what's left of the food in the pantry, what you don't want I'll take or dump,' she heard Rod say.

'No thanks. Jerry wouldn't touch it. There is no way I can say I bought it, it's far too extravagant for his tastes and if I admitted I pinched it, well he'd see that as a crime, he would be horrified and try to make me give it back.'

'Well that's it then. No problem I'll find a home for it. It's time to go.'

Lisa realised she had made a dreadful mistake. The couple were seconds from coming out of the kitchen and there was not time to get back to the bedroom. She looked at the cellar door under the stairs with the key protruding from the lock. It took her two seconds to reach it and open the door, step in and close the door behind her before the couple emerged from the kitchen. She stood on the top step of a steep flight of stairs which ran down to a wine cellar. She heard the front door open and close. After a few minutes a car door slammed and there was a burst from a car horn, and then another car engine and another slammed car door. She opened the door a few inches and poked her head out cautiously. She almost fainted when she realised there was someone outside the front door and the door was being pushed open. She managed to close the cellar door just before Rod came back into the hall. He came directly to the cellar and turned the door latch. Lisa held her breath sure the game was up. There was no way to talk her way out of this one. But by some miracle the door stayed closed.

She had been holding her breath and took a gulp of air. It was with a sigh of relief she heard the front door slam again and a car drive away. She could not understand what had just happened. But when she tried to open the cellar door the reason became horribly clear. The door had been locked from the other side. It was an old type of lock with a retro keyhole. She put her eye to it and could see that the key had gone. She turned the door handle futilely, bashed her shoulder hopelessly into the door. She was trapped in the wine cellar and there was no way out. She looked around the room, saw bottles of expensive, rare, vintage wines resting in racks and a small table, which was probably for tastings. A row of long-stemmed, wide-bowled glasses hung from a rack, and a variety of corkscrews and other bottle openers were arrayed on a shelf. There was no window. She shivered, it was unusually cold, she realised the cellar must be air conditioned and as there was no control panel in the cellar that she could see, it must be outside in the hall. As a means of protecting the wine, the temperature must have been set to almost freezing. She rubbed her bare arms. The thin cotton dress would not keep her warm. Lisa put her head in her hands and felt despair try to invade her soul. She curled up into a foetal position, hid her face in the folds of her dress and breathed in the ripe smell of Bliss.

When Rod had left the house the first time and driven off in his Land Rover, which had photographs of his smiling, trust-worthy face printed along both sides and carried the slogan, "*Rodney Miles – Bespoke Realtor – Exceptional properties for exceptional people,*" he had not gone very far before something

 Brian Millard

had occurred to him that entailed a three-point turn across the road and a trip back to the house. He had remembered the key he had left for Chrissie to get into the house if she was there before him would still be where she had returned it, under the flower pot. He had put it there simply to prevent the possibility of her waiting for him sitting in her car. The previous week she had had waited for him and had been furious, threatening to drive home should it happen again. Leaving a key in such an obvious spot was not something he was comfortable doing but as the job had come to an end and he would not be absent for long, he had taken a chance. Something else had been nagging him too, the cellar door he felt sure had not been locked. He had gone back into the house, collected the key from under the flower pot, locked the cellar door and left, taking the cellar key with him.

More than a week later he was back to oversee the removal of the furniture and props, supervise the thorough cleaning of the place and also ensure a new modern security system was installed to replace the defunct old one. He had no need to go into the cellar. The air conditioning control still read eight degrees. He drove home at the end of the day feeling he had done a professional job and had earned his extremely high commission.

When the day came to hand over the keys to the new owners both he and Chrissie were there to celebrate with their clients. They waited outside on the pebble drive until the Bentley carrying the diminutive figure of Big Boris, a ravishing Tatiana and the two thugs posing as chauffeur and man servant appeared. (The term *Big,* bestowed as a joke by Rod, was used to describe the rather short, smooth faced, and weak chinned Russian multi billionaire). Once inside the house a magnum of champagne was opened and poured. Glasses in hand, the group wandered around the house, inspecting the condition and the new security system. They all trooped down into the cellar to check out the vintage wines. The bodyguards led the way, making a show of being prepared for the worst, adopted the posture and movements of a military hard entry, all they needed were Glock pistols pointing to the ceiling. The performance was threatening and disconcerting. When they reached the bottom of the steps, the chauffeur stopped and, with the flat of his hand, indicated those behind him should stay where they were. The other thug turned and made a couple of strange signs with his fingers. He crouched and shot into the cellar, peering suspiciously into every gloomy corner. When satisfied his boss had nothing to fear, he stood flat against the wall and indicted the rest of the group could descend.

Rod could hardly contain himself and almost burst out laughing. He wondered what on earth they were expecting to find down here. Hidden assassins perhaps or a body in advanced stages of decay? But as he also reached the bottom of the steps he detected a pungent odour that did not belong. Surreptitiously he tried to follow the scent in an attempt to find where it emanated. Then he recognised what it was. It was something he had smelt before and it was unmistakeable. He could detect the lingering scent of Bliss.

Chrissie was well underway with one of her self-deprecating charm offensives. She was claiming to Big Boris that she knew nothing about wine. Rod smiled, there were few top wines with which Chrissie did not have an intimate relationship. If there was a true wine buff in the room it was she. Rod not wishing to interrupt her, waited until she took a moment to breathe before pulling her aside. 'Can you smell it?' he whispered into her ear. She looked at him bewildered, shrugged exaggeratedly and mouthed 'What?' Rod tried to mime, pointing to the tip of his nose and sniffing the air. Chrissie burst out laughing and turned back to Mr Big and asked innocently, I understand the 'nose' of the wine is one of the ways of identifying the type of soil it was grown in…what do you call it? Is it the 'terroir?'

Big Boris put his nose into his glass and took a deep sniff. 'You are correct, this particular wine I believe, was grown in a limestone subsoil. Being able to identity such things is a skill one learns after long practice.' He looked at Tatiana knowingly. Everyone, with the exception of the two thugs who stood against a wall with arms crossed, joined in sniffing their wine sagely. Game, set and match to Chrissie, thought Rod. He would have to speak to

 Brian Millard

her about the perfume later. Tatiana claimed she was feeling the cold, Rod suggested they re-adjourn elsewhere and led the way back up the flight of brick steps into the warmth of the kitchen.

When Lisa had regained her composure and was able to take stock of her situation she knew she somehow had to get out of the cellar, hyperthermia was a clear and present danger. She first considered calling for help using her cell phone. She tested to see if there was a signal and was relieved to find there was but she could think of no one she dare ask who would be willing and able to break down the front door except the police. A locksmith could get in but might easily report her to the police. Neither option appealed. Her cell phone battery was running low and would need recharging soon. She examined the door and the door frame. Given the tools she believed she could remove the door intact, in its door frame, from the wall. However, after a quick check of the implements used for opening bottles and pulling corks, and knives designed to trim the lead around the cork, she realised they would be of no use whatsoever.

She examined the door lock. She was familiar with most of the older type locks but this one looked even more retro than the ones she had seen her father service or dismantle. There was a flat metal plate over the mechanism, secured by four countersunk screws, which looked as if they had never been removed. She believed that if she could unscrew them and pull away the metal plate she would be able to trip the lock from the inside. It was a simple enough task with a decent screw driver and possibly a squirt of penetrating oil. Lisa could see her father's genial grin and visualised his patient methodical approach to any job of its kind. She went back to the shelf containing the bottle-opening implements and selected a corkscrew-blade combination, a small, sturdy looking knife and a small hand towel. There was a container of dish washing liquid in the sink, she poured a little of it into a glass. An hour later she had shifted two of the screws using the corkscrew to clean around the head of the screw heads and the groove in the heads. She lubricated the screws sparingly with a little dishwashing liquid. The smaller blade being round at the end was of more use than the pointed one on the corkscrew, she ground the end of it on the York stone of the top door step until it resembled a screw driver shape. The grooves in the screw heads were deep and the blade fitted into them well but was in danger of snapping under the pressure needed to loosen the screw. Should it break there were two other similar knives she would utilise if required. With her hands protected by the towel she persevered. Another hour and a half saw the last screw removed. Lisa pried the metal plate free of the lock and the inside workings were revealed. She screwed the mechanism back into place, probed about with the blade, pushed a small lever anti clockwise and the door swung open. She replaced the implements where she had found them, picked up her canvas satchel, looked around her to see if she had forgotten anything and left. The front door locked itself as it swung too.

She took a deep breath and jogged to her car which she had left parked half a mile away and drove carefully home.

A few weeks later Lisa presented her dissertation in good time for appraisal. I was well received by the adjudicators who applauded her thorough research and originality. There were parts in it that raised the eyebrows of one tutor but she made no comment other than to say it was 'most interesting.' She was subsequently awarded a masters degree in anthropology and obtained her PhD. Some months later having rejected a few offers of employment by various commercial entities she accepted a position with a 'not for profit' Government funded enterprise which entailed an overseas posting to Uganda. She was to study and report on traditional beliefs, ethnicity and their perceived power on female sexual behaviour.

To celebrate she decided to splash out and for the first time ever indulged her femineity. Her first purchase was a facial and a new hairstyle. She then bought, after long deliberation, a pair of sling-back Jimmy Choo sandals

 Brian Millard

and a wrap around tie-belted camel hair overcoat with a very broad collar
designed by Stella McCartney.

The last portrait

London 1949

Nadja Pasternak had been in Great Britain for more than four years before she met the Polish artist Feliks Topolski. They were drawn to each other at a gathering of Polish émigrés in Hammersmith.

West London then was teeming with many ethnic groups from war torn Europe and favoured by Poles for its proximity to St Andrew Bobola Roman Catholic Church. It had been some time since she had spoken in Polish and in no time at all she was pouring her heart out to him. She was lonely and desperate for a shoulder to cry on. She had left Poland and her loving family for London to study at the Royal Academy School of Music.

Nadja had been extremely lucky to leave the small village on the outskirts of Krakow where she was born, when she did. A few months later, Nazi Germany invaded Poland. She learnt whilst in London that German troops had overrun the capital Krakow. The family home was in nearby rural Feliksen. Nadja had no knowledge of what might have befallen her parents and younger sister. The last time she had seen them was at the railway station in Krakow, when they stood waving to her through billowing steam as the train pulled away. Her father was a highly skilled maker of string instruments. He had made the cello and violin she had carried with her from Poland. His life savings willingly spent to further her education. Each night since then she had prayed for their safety.

Topolski listened patiently. He appreciated her loneliness and her concern for her family. He was prepared to help in any way he could, she was obviously struggling and short of money. He was already well established in the British art scene and had a wide circle of influential friends and patrons. He was happy to introduce her to people who might open new doors for her. He suspected she might well be offended if he offered to give her money more directly. But he was prepared to do so if requested. It was the least he could do for a fellow Pole. He was attracted to Nadja for a variety of reasons, not the least of which was her physical beauty. She was tall and elegant and carried herself gracefully. Her features could be described as classic, high cheek bones, strong chin and fine skin possibly a little on the pale, side set off by the bluest of blue lapis lazuli eyes and framed by long lustrous dark hair, one errant lock of which fell tantalizingly across an eye. He admired her obvious passion for music and also her courage. He was sure when playing her cello she was a sight to behold. She would make an excellent model. The informal social group of expat Poles met monthly. They arranged to look out for one another at the next meeting.

When Topolski and Nadja saw each other again he had a proposal for her. He had spoken to his acquaintance the artist Francis Bacon about her and suggested he introduce her to him over lunch the following week. He made no mention of the possibility of work as a model. The meeting would be simply a means of expanding her circle of acquaintances. Nadja agreed graciously, a free lunch would be more than welcome. She was formally introduced to Francis Bacon at Wheelers Oyster Bar in old Compton Street. She found him charming, alarming and disarming.

One look was enough for Bacon to demand she sit for him. Nadja embarrassed and uncertain as to what this entailed listened silently and then politely declined. Wine was served then followed by oysters on the shell. These were quickly despatched by the gentlemen, Nadja looked on not sure if she should try one or not, did nothing. Topolski adroitly changed the subject to Bacon's work. Bacon needing no encouragement to talk about himself, expounded at length.

  Brian Millard

'I want my paintings to leave a trail of the human presence and memory. A trace of past events as a snail leaves its slime.'

Nadja somewhat perturbed, sipped her wine wide eyed. 'I have always been very moved by pictures of slaughterhouses,' Bacon claimed. He gazed at Nadja serenely 'If I go into a butcher's shop, I always think it surprising that I wasn't there instead of the animal'.

A plate of steaming rare beef appeared before him. He tucked in with relish. 'You should meet Lucian.' Nadja looked at Topolski with alarm. Did the man wish her to meet a butcher she wondered?

A similar plate of roast beef and vegetables was set before her and was quickly despatched

Addressing Topolski, Bacon said, 'What say you, Feliks?'

'Yes I agree,' Topolski said.

'May I ask who this gentleman is you wish me to meet?'

'Lucian Freud, my dear girl,' he said. 'He's teaching at the Slade. He paints the human form too. I think you would find him most interesting. He and Francis are the closest of friends.'

Francis Bacon raised an eyebrow archly as if to say, 'You can say that again.'

The meal came to an end. As they stood to leave, showing a complete disregard for the amount, Bacon showered the table with bank notes which fluttered down like a flock of birds. Nadja estimated she could live on the amount for more than two months. At the time Bacon was in his early thirties and opening homosexual, his fame as an artist growing apace with his reputation for reckless gambling and debauchery. He was profligate when in funds and already an alcoholic.

'Onwards to the Gargoyle,' he announced.

Topolski took Nadja's arm and they followed him through the streets to Dean Street and up the stairs to the upper floor of number six. Inside the place was crowded with diners, some dancing to a small jazz combo. Gambling took place on another level of the building, roulette being the most popular way to lose money.

Nadja looked around her, feeling frumpish and uneasy in the sophisticated surroundings. Francis was obviously well-known and seemed on friendly terms with everyone. The waiters showed him extreme deference. He was waved over to other tables on the way to their own, he ordered champagne before he was seated. The first bottle was empted in a flash and quickly replenished. An effete little man with an elegant woman in tow came to the table, planted a kiss on Bacon's lips and settled himself beside him. A waiter brought another chair for the lady, who also sat, appraising Nadja with interest as she did. Topolski introduced her as Simone de Beauvoir.

'Ravie de vous recontrer,' Simone de Beauvoir murmured, offering Nadja a gloved hand.

'And this is her husband Jean Paul Sartre,' said Topolski.

Sartre took Nadja's hand and said, 'Enchante.' Nadja retrieved it quickly.

A strikingly beautiful young man appeared from the staircase. He was not tall but his posture and self assurance gave him the appearance of a much taller man. He had fair hair, prominent high cheek bones and a strong aquiline nose. He came up to Sartre and put a hand on his shoulder. Simone stood and embraced the young man passionately. 'How much did you lose?' she asked.

'A great deal but it is no concern. It's good to win,' he said, 'but better to lose.'

Simone de Beauvoir threw up her arms exclaiming 'Incorrigible, how can losing be better than winning?

'To lose money is an incentive to work harder in order to get more,' he smiled.

'And this is Lucian Freud, the other enfant terrible of the art world,' said Topolski.'

Lucian Freud bowed ceremoniously then kissed each member of the party in the French manner, on both cheeks, with the exception of Nadja. When he reached her they shook hands. He held her hand for longer than was polite, looking intensely into her face, studying her in detail.

 Brian Millard

More champagne was ordered, Sartre and Bacon danced together. Simone attempted to engage Nadja in conversation in French with little success. Topolski interpreted in Polish and English. Nadja became acutely aware of Freud's eyes burning into her. They seemed to penetrate her soul, so unrelenting was his gaze. She lowered her eyes, toyed with her champagne glass but when she looked up his eyes had not moved. She felt like a butterfly under a microscope. She stood and told Topolski she had to leave.

She had to pass Lucian's chair to do so, as she did he caught her hand, looked up to her with a smile and completely disarmed her by insisting Topolski bring her to meet his wife at his studio as soon as possible. He refused to take no for an answer. He claimed he would appreciate her opinion of his current work. Nadja decided there was something decidedly otherworldly about him, he possessed an indefinable quality she found impossible to put into words but so intrigued was she that she found herself agreeing. A time and date were arranged.

When the day came Topolski dutifully collected her from her lodgings and delivered her to Freud's home and studio in Paddington. To her relief, Francis Bacon was there, talking animatedly to a person who she learnt was another artist and a friend of the host. His name was Leon Scully. He was a personable young man whose manner seemed to be direct to the point of being rude. He seemed to speak without thinking, yet his observations she found refreshingly innocent and often funny. She could not place his accent. She liked his short trimmed beard, as well as his forthright manner.

Lucian Freud was married to Kitty Godley the daughter of Jacob Epstein. She was a celebrated beauty and the subject of a series of paintings by Freud. She appeared from a kitchen carrying a tray with a coffee pot and cups. She was introduced to Nadja and embraced her.

'But my dear,' she said, you are positively beautiful. Lucian told me you were Polish, but he never mentioned your exquisite eyes.' In fact it was Kitty's own incredibly large eyes that dominated the portraits that would immortalise her.

Then Lucian made his entrance. He was naked to the waist except for a long scarf thrown rakishly around his throat. Tied around his waist was what looked like an old sheet pulled from his bed. He cast an eye around the room. 'Ah! Scully, good to see you, are you ready to paint? And Feliks, perhaps you'd care to join in too?' Scully appeared bemused and good-humouredly indicated his pallet and brushes on a table nearby, inviting Topolski to take his place. Topolski shook his head, claiming he had a prearranged appointment with a gallery owner.

'No painting for me today old chap,' he said. 'I am strictly on escort duty.'

Lucian grinning said 'I take it you have all met our model, Nadja.' He gestured theatrically to Nadja.

Nadja stood up and immediately headed for the door. Topolski shamefaced, attempted to restrain her. 'Nadja, I had no idea,' he bleated. He turned to Freud, 'Lucian this is really too much, you have brought the poor girl here under false pretences.'

Kitty also turned on her husband. 'How could you? She went to Nadja and put her arm around her shoulders.

'He told me he wanted my opinion on his work.'

'And so I do.' Lucian said without a qualm. 'But where's the harm in asking you to sit for us. For goodness sake, it's not as if we expect you to pose naked. Just as you are is perfect. It will only be for an hour or two.'

Scully no longer amused said, 'Lucian if the lady does not wish to pose, I see no reason why she or I for that matter, need to be here. So if it's all the same to you...'

'Don't listen to Leon', Lucian interrupted 'He's from the Antipodes, Australia or some other God forsaken place.

'New Zealand as a matter of fact,' Leon said, smiling at Nadja.

Everyone looked at Nadja. 'Will Kitty be here?' she asked.

'Of course she will,' said Lucian reassuringly. 'Won't you Darling?' Kitty shook her head despairingly, shrugged and began to gather up the coffee

                    Brian Millard

things. She nodded approval to Nadja and smiled. 'He means no harm, it's just his way.'

'Very well,' said Nadja cautiously.

'Now if that's all settled, I'll leave you to it and return for Nadja in, shall we say, an hour and a half or so,' said Topolski. 'I assure you you have nothing to fear from these fellows, my dear girl. I can personally vouch for Leon. He is an honourable fellow, even if a trifle gauche. Lucian is a married man and Francis as queer as a ten bob note.' And with that Topolski made for the door leaving Nadja looking like a startled fawn.

'Well gentlemen, this is by way of an occasion,' announced Lucian. 'Until now I have always sat down to paint. I have found my work somewhat lacking a sense of spontaneity, as a result. So I have decided to take a leaf out of my dear friend Francis's book and stand to paint from now on. I have no intention of emulating his style but simply intend to loosen both my corsets and my stroke and hopefully create a more gestural effect. So chaps this will be my last painting in the old manner and definitely my last portrait sitting down. You may of course stand or sit as you wish. After today I will kick away my chair and work on my feet. This will be my last portrait sitting down. '

'Nadja please sit here on this couch, do not adopt a pose. Simply relax. If you need to move, you may do so.'

Nadja did as instructed and tried to relax but without a great deal of success. She watched with interest as each artist arranged their work surfaces and began to work. Scully shifted his position a couple of times and then with charcoal began drawing a small design a few inches square in a thinly applied monochrome at the top right corner of his canvas, rubbing out with his finger and adjusting as he saw fit and measuring proportions with a paint brush, smiling at her as he did. He appeared completely at ease and unhurried.

Bacon's approach could not have been more different. He barely looked at her. He squirted paint from the tube directly onto the reverse, un-primed side of the canvas and scrubbed at it with a brush, slapped on more pigment of different hues and worked them together with his fingers. Occasionally he made a violent brushstroke followed by foul cursing and frenzied rubbing with a turps soaked rag. He seemed to literally attack the canvas as if it was a foe he had to defeat. Splatters of oil paint flew about with abandon. Fortunately none reached Nadja.

Freud did little but glare at her. His intense scrutiny, it seemed to Nadja, continued for an inordinate length of time. She was relieved when he finally turned to his easel and proceeded to clean his brushes leisurely, seemingly completely indifferent to the concentrated activity of his companions. Whilst so occupied, he recited poetry. He launched into a poem by Auden, then another by TS Elliot, followed by a word-perfect Shakespearean sonnet. His performance concluded with a lewd limerick.

> *'While Titian was mixing Rose Madder*
> *His model reclined on a ladder*
> *The position to Titian*
> *Suggested coition,*
> *So he ran up the ladder and had her.'*

This raised a snigger from Bacon. Freud was not finished. As an encore, he burst into song with a selection of operatic arias, delivered in a strong and pleasing baritone. Freud was not simply attempting to entertain, his intention was to relax the model and make mental notes of the changes in her expression and posture.

Nadja fortunately had not understood a great deal of the bard's words and even less of the limerick, applauded the singing tentatively. Scully joined her by stamping his feet and crying, 'Bravo, Bravo!' Scully had continued painting quietly without comment or lack of concentration.

'Enough, I'm done, I need a drink. That's it,' said Bacon and, leaving the shambles he had created as it was, strode out of the door. Bacon had

     Brian Millard

recently made a major sale and on the proceeds had moved into a studio at seven Cromwell Place once owned by the pre-Raphaelite Millais. Bacon now resided there with his former nanny, who not only looked after him but bizarrely assisted him in running an elicit roulette club from the premises. She apparently had a preference for sleeping on the kitchen table.

When Topolski turned up to collect his charge, he found Freud deeply involved in painting and Scully having produced a fine looking, almost completed painting, cleaning his brushes. Nadja now appeared perfectly relaxed and at ease and in no need of being rescued. He waited for a while but was genuinely anxious to get away. He was acutely aware of Lucian's habit of painting through the night when he felt like it. He asked him how much longer he anticipated the session would take. Lucian ignored him. It took Scully to suggest he take Nadja home in his stead. Nadja nodded and smiled her thanks. Topolski was relieved and went his way leaving Nadja in Scully's care.

Shortly afterwards Scully too was ready to leave. Nadja stood and stretched. Scully's painting was wet and difficult to transport so he left it where it was. He told Lucian he would arrange for it to be collected. If Freud was aware of what he had said or not, he made no response. Leon and Nadja left together leaving him working seemingly oblivious to anything else.

Leon Scully was born in New Zealand. He was more than a decade older than Nadja. He had been painting professionally for twenty years. His reputation was established and like Bacon he had recently moved to the Hanover Gallery. He had been with The House of Assario for some time but had been persuaded to make the change when Bacon moved. Assario was well established but had proved lax in keeping up with the trends. The proprietor had tried to promote his work but sales of late had tailed off. Scully's work was in the vanguard of the fast growing popularity for figurative expressionist paintings. He had left New Zealand to escape the stifling resistance to change by the art establishment. He had begun to feel frustrated in a similar manner with Assario.

Most heterosexual men were physically attracted to Nadja and Leon was no exception. His good fortune was that Nadja was similarly attracted to him. From their first meeting in Freud's studio he had decided to pursue her romantically. Nadja found his attention flattering, his humour and positive attitude appealing. The first meal they shared at the Cafe Royal gave her a taste for what London could offer. It took only once for Leon to hear her play her cello, for him to be totally committed. When Nadja left the Royal Academy of music and found a place with the London Symphony Orchestra, he never missed a performance. It was an idyllic time for them both. The only thing to mar their days was the uncertainty of what had happened to her family in Poland. They were married at the St Andrew Bobola Roman Catholic Church in Hammersmith. Topolski was best man.

Auckland, New Zealand. The present.

Francesca Symonds had just returned home from taking their daughter to primary school. Grey Lynn was leafy and peaceful at this hour of the morning. It was almost time to meet her husband Richard for coffee in nearby Ponsonby when her cell beeped. The call was from Richard who claimed he had something of interest to tell her. He needed to make a couple of calls before he could explain exactly what it was about.

She found him talking on his cell, sitting in their usual spot in the shade of an umbrella outside the cafe. He waved hello, and she kissed him in between sentences as he continued speaking into his cellphone.

'So Andrew, can you run this by me one more time, slowly please. As I understand it, a painting that may or may not be kosher has been offered for auction, and there is some doubt as to its prominence? Right what would you like me to do specifically? … Is that absolutely necessary? I see, I take it it will be at my usual daily rate. The person on the line went into a lengthy spiel

 Brian Millard

and Richard whispered to Fran 'You need to hear this firsthand,' he raised his eyebrows and she shrugged. 'Do I build the flight and accommodation into my costs, or will Christies take care of it? I see. Business class, yes? And is it absolutely essential for Fran to be there as well?' This prompted Fran to put her hands palms down and scissor them back and forth to indicate no. 'I see,' continued Richard. 'Well who knows what the job will entail, hopefully it won't be necessary. I'll get back to you with a ball park estimate as soon as you put your proposal in writing. I have Fran here beside me, would you like to speak to her?' Fran now looked even more alarmed. 'Sorry she's up to her neck in something best not to bother her. Yes I will. Ok, I'll look forward to it.' Richard closed down his cell as their coffees arrived, a latte for Fran and a long black for Richard. 'That was Andrew from Christies in London he wants me to fly out, business class, to London.'

'So I gather,' Fran said flatly as Richard drank some of his long black, pursed his lips and squinted into the sun, then added some hot water to the tiny cup. 'And…?'

Richard looked at his wife 'And what?'

'And, is that it? What about your loving family? It's your daughter's birthday next week or have you forgotten?'

'Me forget? Of course not, she'll be, ah, five next Sunday.'

'And what did you agree to do next Sunday?'

'Mmm… yes, a birthday treat wasn't it? Now let me see. Ah yes, Kelly Talton's and the penguins. I am to take her and her friend, forget her name, to see the penguins being fed. Now you'll have to help me here, at what time do the birds in tuxedos eat? It's slipped my mind.

'Hopeless, absolutely hopeless, really I despair. I can't be your live-in PA.

'It will come to me or I'll Google it. No big deal.'

'You do intend to keep your promise I hope.'

'Naturally, I said I would do it, so I will. I'll be back with time to spare.'

'Make sure you are'.

'There is one thing'.

'Why am I not surprised?'

'It seems your talents will be needed too. How do you fancy a few days in London in a good hotel, all found, including Business Class flights?'

'You really are an absolute bastard Richard.' Fran thought for a few minutes. 'You'd better tell me what dear Andrew is up to and why he can afford to throw Christie's money about like this.'

'Later Darling let's just enjoy our coffee. There should be a proposal winging its way to me in an hour or so. Just think of it, London in late spring. Daffodils in Hyde Park, a boat trip on the Thames to the Tate Modern, Lunch on the South Bank and dinner at Claridges, all on expenses. Oh yes most appealing.'

Fran bit her lip. 'Don't count your chickens Dude'.

By the following morning there was a text in Richard's inbox from Christies with a proposal attached. Richard printed it off and read whilst he ate his breakfast cornflakes. His five year old daughter Emily sat beside him doing the same and ignoring him. Like Fran he had wondered why Christies were prepared to fund his involvement. He learnt that in fact the exercise would cost the auction house nothing, and the vendor would be footing the bill. The vendor was a well established dealer gallery with a long pedigree with whom he was familiar called Assario Fine Arts. For reasons which were undisclosed Christies had stipulated the painting be expertly examined and bona fides confirmed before they would be prepared to accept the paintings for auction. This Richard found interesting and although it rang a warning bell he was intrigued. Obviously provenance was in question. He recalled that the owner of Assario Fine Arts with whom he had dealings had died a few years ago. He wondered who had taken over.? It had always been a family owned business representing a stable of first tier name artists and was considered most reputable and reliable.

Richard buttered a slice of toast and enquired of Emily if she would prefer Vegemite or marmalade. Fran appeared, still damp from the shower, and promptly stuffed a table napkin around her daughter's neck, picked up

 Brian Millard

the buttered toast and smeared it with Vegemite. 'Vegemite for you, young lady,' she said. 'Is that the proposal from Andrew?'

'Darling, you'll need to read it.' Fran reached for the document, skimmed through it quickly whilst smearing a generous amount of marmalade on the remaining toast. Emily and Richard shared a 'what can you do look'. Fran, still eating stood and took her daughter's hand. 'Lunch box, school bag, Gym togs?' she listed.

'All in school bag', added Emily smirking.

'Well done. Then let's go girl'.

'See you for coffee, usual place?'

'Order me a flat white and we'll talk,' she said indicating the printout.

Deal,' said Richard.

Doctor Richard Symonds was always keen to have a break from his regular job as a senior lecturer at Auckland University. He was an art professional of long standing and considered by the academic world to be an expert on art history from the Renaissance to the present and the leading world authority on the work of NZ artist Leon Scully. He was the chair of the Katya Trust and curator of Leon Scully's entire work. He and Fran had been instrumental in the discovery of fifty unknown works by Scully, all portraits of a female muse. The discovery brought Scully back to the public's attention and restored his reputation in his homeland, where previously he had been ignored. Books, television documentaries and lecture tours followed the discovery. Already accustomed to being called as an expert witness in a courtroom, or to give independent valuation advice or to solve issues of provenance, Richard became even more respected and in demand. Fran was also an art professional specialising in research and forensics but with a personal interest in political and social issues involving art in the contemporary scene. She too was well published. Her work on indigenous Māori art, its appropriation and the moral aspects of contemporary art had also found their way into print. Fran now worked from home purely to give their daughter the childhood she believed she deserved. But the time was fast approaching when Emily's needs would no longer take so much priority.

She found Richard sitting waiting for her at their usual table outside their favourite coffee shop in Ponsonby. She slumped down opposite him. 'Why do women drive those great big hum-vees? I simply can't see the point of them. They park them in ludicrous places, totally ignore the signs, leave them in front of drives or so close to little cars like mine it's impossible to move and then you have to wait for them to come and shift it.' The waitress delivered their coffees with a smile.

'You look like you need this Fran,' she said 'might be time for a little me time.'

'Thanks Shania. Where would we be without you and your smile?'

'Well there you are, I'm not the only one who thinks you need a break,' said Richard.

'The traffic is even worse in London.'

'It's different when you are sitting in one of those beautiful old black London cabs.'

'It's not that I don't want to come with you, we *are* both in need of a break. The only time we seem to spend together is here or when we take the boat out to the island for a meeting with the board of trustees. And that is still business related. It's not just *me* time it's *us* time that we need.'

'I agree. We do need more 'us' time but Emily has to come first.'

'Sometimes Richard, I realise just how lucky we are to have each other and to be a family. It will not be the same for ever but she is all we have and I don't want to waste a second of her growing up.'

'Of course, you are right, which is why I have checked out the cost of flights for children. It will soon be the school holidays. We can easily afford it and Emily would love it. She needs to experience the world outside of her own. It will be educational as well as fun'

'Are you sure we will be paid?'

'Yes we will be paid, it is contractual.'

    Brian Millard

'Oh now I don't know what to think. Let me look at the proposal again. Either way you must go. It's probably wiser for Emily and me to follow a little later. That is we go too. Do you honestly think it could work?'

'We'll make it work.'

'Look I'm being silly, there's absolutely no point in us travelling separately.'

'Of course there isn't.'

London, a week later.

The Symonds family arrived at Heathrow feeling surprisingly fresh and alert. They had each enjoyed a good eight hours sleep and a short nap before the aircraft began to descend. Andrew as promised was there to meet them as they emerged from customs. They were soon seated in his electric Lexus gliding silently through tunnels and along motorways into central London. Little Emily felt her eyes grow heavy and in a short while was asleep in her mother's arms. This didn't stop her parents engaging Andrew in small talk, catching up with what was happening in their friend's life.

They asked after Wendy his wife and their two daughters, one was about Emily's age, Sam, for Samantha and the other a little more than a year older, called Bobby for Roberta. 'All's well you know, tootling along as usual,' he claimed and shrugged. He became much more articulate, even excited, when asked how his work was going, 'The art market has never been better. Not just buoyant but blooming booming,' he exclaimed. 'Prices are climbing to levels we on the shop floor considered impossible a few years ago, long may it last.'

'Yes indeed.'

They were soon in Mayfair, the Lexus parked neatly outside Claridges Hotel and a porter was busy loading their bags onto a trolley. Richard agreed to pop over to St James's Park that afternoon to be briefed. They waved as Andrew drove off.

Emily awoke as her father carried her into the impressive foyer of marble and gilt, glittering chandeliers and unbridled luxury, her eyes open as wide as were her mother's.

After lunch Fran announced that she and Emily would be taking a walk in Hyde Park and make an initial inspection of their immediate surroundings. It was only a short distance to Buckingham Palace. Emily wondered if the Queen would be in. 'Well if she is she might give you a cup of tea and a chocolate chip biscuit,' Richard said. They would keep in touch by cell, fresh air and a leisurely few hours was the order for the rest of the day. Richard walked in the park too, cutting across to Christies in St James.

'Sorry if I have seemed less than forthcoming in our communications to date, Richard, but when you are presented with two previously totally unknown paintings claimed to be by artists who have fetched bids in the many millions, one is best to be a little cautious with one's opinions. The last Bacon that went under the hammer fetched a cool nine million pounds, and Freud actually surpassed that by several more.'

'Andrew is it possible for me to see, if not necessarily examine these painting, now?

'Sorry. Not the actually paintings but I do have, quite illegitimately, images of them on my cell phone. Before the vendor brought them in he sent the images. We of course requested we view the paintings and even then stipulated that they undergo evaluation by a specialist such as you.

'I was wondering why you chose me for the job, surely there was someone local you could have used and saved airfares and hotel bills?'

'The reason it had to be you and Francesca, Richard, will become self evident after you see the images. Here they are.' Andrew handed Richard his cell. Richard made the image as large as possible and saw what at first glance what could be an unfinished work by Francis Bacon. He scrolled down and did the same with the second image. He studied it for some time.

 Brian Millard

'Right, now I see where you are coming from Andy, and why it had to be me.'

'Guilty as charged. So what do you think?'

'Well take the one claimed to be by Bacon. It's hard to come to any conclusions without having it your hands. I must reserve judgement until after Xrays and so forth are complete. There is a possibility that it could be the real thing. But don't quote me on this I could easily be wrong'

'And the one claimed to be a Freud?'

'Well, Initially I thought it could be an early one, something he might have done prior to his change of style and process. His early works up to the fifties were painted rather thinly and somewhat tightly, the exaggerated eyes were a forerunner to what came later which was of course his obsessive scrutiny and focus on whatever characteristic he felt was the essence of the individual. Here there is only a slight exaggeration in the model's features. The mouth has sensuality and the demeanour shows a degree of anxiety. About this time he abandoned sable brushes and detail and developed his images by constant layering and scumbling with stiff bristle brushes, the strokes sweeping and looping, virtually drawing in paint. But then this is the reason you brought me here, isn't Andy?'

'It is.'

'Have you any idea who the model is?'

'Well I have a suspicion as you have guessed'

'It bears a resemblance to a lady of Polish descent who became Leon Scully's wife. When do I get to see the originals?'

'We have an appointment this afternoon with the vendor. He has been, shall we say, less than forthcoming with regards to how and why he actually has them in his possession. You will be familiar with the company. It is Assario, now run by the younger son Tony.' His father Edwin, as you know, died almost two years ago.'

'Is it still a family trust?'

'Yes but the family involvement has shifted in other directions. They have interests in several other industries. The grandfather was the real thing and had a stable of many of the top artists of the day. We are talking about artists such as Graham Sutherland, Feliks Topolski and, of course, Bacon and Freud. But when the grandfather died and the business passed to Edwin things began to change. Many of the best artists departed, Sutherland, Bacon, Freud then Scully all went over to Hanover. This would have been about nineteen forty seven or eight, even later. Edwin was an honest dealer and did his best to nurture his artists. He sustained good relationships on the social level with his clients but he did not have the flair, humour or charm of the founder. He was a meticulous bookkeeper but his relationships tended to be more functional than personal, and now, since Edwin has departed the scene, his son has taken over the day to day running of the fine arts side.'

'I'll text Fran and tell her where I will be.'

Fran and Emily had fed ducks on the Serpentine, been entranced by a troop of horse guards riding in formation through the park and wandered down the Mall to the gates outside the palace. Emily fascinated by everything she saw, recorded it all digitally on her personal IPad and constantly sent the images winging off to her best friend Izzy back in New Zealand. Fran read Richard's text, and immediately texted him back. She wished him good luck and assured him they were enjoying themselves, although sadly the Queen was not receiving guests that day. In lieu of tea and biscuits they were off to find ice cream instead.

Tony Assario kept Richard and Andrew waiting for nearly fifteen minutes. His receptionist, a strikingly good looking young woman wearing tight jeans and an overlong sweater-cum jacket, having informed her boss of their arrival had lapsed into silence and pretended to busy herself with her computer.

Tony Assario came down a flight of curved metal stairs and apologised profusely for having to keep them waiting. He offered them coffee which they declined. He was below average height, his hair shaved on either side well above the ears, a shock of dark hair stood stiffly to attention on the top. He was wearing a dark pinstripe suite, a sheer white silk shirt, a pair of white Nikes and no socks. He indicated a black, glass topped coffee table supported on spindly metal legs and asked them sit down in equally precarious looking leather chairs around it. He offered them coffee which they declined. Introductions were made.

'Well, gentlemen, here we are,' he said. 'I trust you had a good flight Doctor Symonds. Is the accommodation to your liking?'

'No complaints on either account, thank you.'

'Shall we get down to business?' asked Andrew.

'By all means,' Toni Assario waved his assistant over. 'On my desk there is a package containing two precious works of art. Please bring them here Fiona.' The girl dutifully disappeared up the twisting staircase. 'As you will see there have been a few changes here at Assario. But the same level of integrity initiated by my grandfather, Noah, nearly a century ago, still prevails. We have changed with the times, as one must, to meet the challenges of a vastly different art scene. Now that my father Edwin is no longer with us it has come to me to continue his legacy of nurturing new talent and cementing relationships with new patrons. One could say our positioning has changed but the brand has remained constant.

'Ah, here's Fiona with the paintings. Thanks babe.' He took the parcel from her and placed it, with reverence, in the centre of the coffee table. It was wrapped in Assario wrapping paper printed with a step and repeat design of the company logo. The logo was in gold against a rich dark green background. The parcel had been sealed originally by a printed sticker, which also displayed the company logo. 'Amazingly we are still using the very same design as our corporate identity after nearly a century. Try as I may to make even minor changes to it, they incur the wrath of God from the family. It was designed by grandfather you see.' He removed the wrapping paper and it fell to the floor. Richard idly picked it up and examined it closely, he noticed a scrawled note in what looked like calligraphic handwriting, but it was so faded and dusty he could not determine the words.

'May I?' Richard asked but without waiting for permission picked up the top painting lying face down over the other. It was an oil painting on canvas which had been taped tightly on board. Richard carefully lifted a corner of the tape to reveal un-primed brown canvas. He wet his finger and gently rubbed dirt from the edge of the painting surface. He took out from his jacket pocket a loupe magnifying eye piece, placed it over the area he had wet and looked through it intently. He did the same in another spot. He pulled out a note book and wrote something into it. And without a word placed both note book and eye piece back in his inside pocket.

'Well Doctor, is it a Bacon or not?' Tony Assario asked eagerly. Richard ignored him, set the first painting aside and picked up the other.

Of the two paintings, this was the one in which he was most interested. It was painted on a stretched canvas and was little more than thinly applied oil washes over pencil. The original pencil marks had in several areas been left untouched by pigment. The palette was limited to three or four colours and applied Ala Prima. As a result the strokes could be discerned clearly. The colours were neutrals made from the primary major triad. It depicted a female, possibly in her late twenties, wearing a long-sleeved cotton or silk blouse, which is buttoned to the neck. There is a bemused expression on her face, her eyebrows raised but the large very blue eyes are sad, tired and introspective. This is an intelligent face, the lips full, her hair shoulder- length and dark, an errant lock of hair falls across a high brow. She is a beautiful woman. Most of the background is left white, save for the faint indication of arm in faded pencil and the beginnings of a single stroke of rich background shadow behind the head.

Richard placed the painting beside the other. Took out his note book again and spent some time writing in it.

'Well?' Tony Assario asked impatiently. It's a Freud, am I right?

      Brian Millard

Richard felt his hackles rise but still did not reply, he continued making notes. He slid his note pad into his inside pocket, lent forward, steepled his fingers and smiled.

'You will realise Mr Assario that I am not at liberty to give an opinion at this stage, it's far too early in the process. I will need to take the paintings away and have them X-rayed today. If you wish you may accompany us to see them safely delivered, but they will be out of your hands for at least most of this week in any event. I will work with the forensic team at their premises. If you wish I am sure Christies would be happy to sign something to this effect.'

'Normal protocol, type it up and I will sign a receipt. No probs,' said Andrew.

'Well if you say so,' said Assario. 'There is a great deal of money at stake here. Fiona could you re package these paintings in clean wrapping paper?'

'That won't be necessary said Richard quickly. Please leave them in the original wrappings.'

'Oh well if you say so,' said Tony Assario.

Fiona typed out a receipt as Andrew dictated. : *"Two unsigned paintings by unknown artists, provenance to be ascertained. Released in good faith to the care of Christies Auction House."* The receipt was signed.

Richard carefully rewrapped the paintings and asked for some Sellotape which he used sparingly.

'Before we go Mr Assario Would you mind answering a couple of questions of a chronological nature.'

'Sure but please call me Tony.'

'Very well, I dislike being called Doctor, it sounds so pompous. Please feel free to call me Richard too.'

'Fire away Richard what would you like to know?'

'How did the paintings came into your possession?' Tony Assario paused and did not answer immediately. He ran a finger across a manicured eyebrow, smiled and sat back.

'That's easy. They were found amongst my Father's things after he passed away.'

'By whom may I ask? Who found them?

'Well I did. I believe my mother was there when I did '

'And exactly where were they discovered?'

'Oh… they were stashed away on top of a cupboard, amongst a stack of old frames and other debris from half a century ago when grandfather was running the show. My father never threw anything away ever.'

'Why do you suppose they were there all this time?'

'Well apart from the fact that they were potentially extremely valuable, I can only suppose that when grandfather started to lose it, he simply forgot they were in stock. And my father probably did not realise the package was there at all or if he did what it contained. Anything else you need to know Richard?'

'That's all, at least for the time being. Well Andy, We must make a move. The offer still stands Tony, if you wish to accompany us to the forensic people to put your mind at ease, you may.'

'No, that won't be necessary Richard. I have things to do here. So when do you think we will know the results?'

'Can I get back to with an exact time-frame? You have yet to meet my partner Francesca. She may well need more information from you whilst I'm busy doing my thing.'

Andrew and Richard shook Tony Assario's limp hand and left, the paintings tucked firmly under Richard's arm.

Andrew had made an appointment with the X-ray Spectrometry Department at the Courtauld Institute of Art. They were met by a pert and attractive middle aged woman and taken to a well lit room set up with a large table for initial examination purposes. The space was absolutely spotless and clinical. They were treated to a tour of the various areas reserved for radiology and infrared technology used for imaging. Richard was impressed by the professionalism and obvious knowledge of the woman and briefed

Brian Millard

her on his requirements. The paintings were examined in a general manner and notes were taken. Andrew, who had been looking on but a little out of his depth, was surprised when Richard smoothed out the wrapping paper and requested a thorough examination of a certain area for indications of handwriting. The paintings were left where they were, arrangements made for a return visit the next day in the afternoon, when most of the exploration would be complete.

Richard and Fran were in bed soon after Emily had closed her eyes. The family would visit London Zoo after breakfast tomorrow but jet lag was taking its toll and for now sleep was the priority.

After breakfast the next day the newly refreshed and energised Symonds family took a black London cab out to Regents Park. Emily as usual was armed with her cell phone and ready to record for posterity, anything and everything new and exciting. Penguins of course were on the agenda as were giraffes and turtles. Richard had to leave them to it in order to get back to St James Square in order to check progress at The Courtauld Institute of Art.

He was met by the same charming woman and listened to her findings. He made the occasional comment asking for clarification when the terminology used was unfamiliar to him. He made copious notes as she spoke and brought up images on the computer screen. The first painting that had been examined was the one thought to be by Bacon.

'We can confirm the date it was painted reasonably accurately as the early nineteen fifties. The materials, canvas, tape, board and pigments, solvents etc were all commensurate with those Bacon was using at this time. The age of the canvas also complies. The gestural nature of the various marks and the directness and speed at which they had been executed has been compared with other works of Bacon's painted at this time, as have the pigments which we have matched from the period with samples held in our pigment archive. The same reduced palette and triads were used.

The examination revealed there was no underpainting. It is painted directly on the reverse side of the un-primed canvas. There are no images obscured by correction. Each stroke was the first and the last. The clincher is the spontaneous smearing and wiping out with a cloth or hand. Hence our conclusion is that the painting most certainly is by Francis Bacon.

As you know he had a habit of being careless with his work, to give them away or forget about them. He would pay off gambling debts with works that in the future might fetch a small fortune. This painting probably fell into this category.'

'Yes he was profligate in quite a few ways, but you know apparently a charming companion, generous and very well read,' Richard commented,' relieved his assumption had been verified.

'Now the painting allegedly by Lucian Freud is a different kettle of fish. The examination revealed the materials used were also commensurate with the time the work was painted. However, the canvas used was of a finer cotton weave than normally used by Freud at the time. The palette also varies from that normally employed by Freud at the time. Freud rarely ever made preliminary drawings or value sketches. He usually began a painting at the focal point and finished that part before moving on. In that sense his paintings were not precisely planned but tended to evolve. His was not a traditional method and as with most things with Freud, convention was ignored.' Ghostly images appeared from below the surface of the top layers of pigment. X-rays reveal underpainting and indicate planning. In the top left corner of the canvas, here, a small preliminary monochrome working design can to seen. It has been painted over with flake white. It shows a well designed composition. It indicates the placement of major shapes. Values have also been clearly established prior to commencement.

'Yes I don't think Freud bothered with any preparatory design quite like this.' Richard said. 'This value sketch may well have been proceeded by several pencil or charcoal drawings of features such as hands or eyes and so forth. It's a rather traditional method and suggests an older more conventional artist. It shows me the artist was deliberately seeking a likeness.

He planned the painting and employed tried and true, if rather conventional means to get there. The composition is well thought out and uses the white of the canvas as an integral component of the design. The placement of the various shapes has a diagonal direction. These are things for which Freud, particularly in this period had scant regard.

'I agree, and as a result we conclude it seems most unlikely that this work came from the brush of Lucian Freud.'

Richard, relieved his personal conclusions and been largely verified, was keen to learn the results of the examination of the wrapping paper. He learnt it had been examined using Ultra Red technology imaging and results were shown to him in close up on the monitor. A strong cursive calligraphic script was revealed and was now perfectly legible.

It read: "Oil Paintings x2. *Property of Francis Bacon and Leon Scully, left for safe keeping March 6 1953 by Feliks Topolski: Artists to collect.*"

'You will be interesting in this area here a white circle appeared around "March 6 1953 by Feliks Topolski." It would appear there has been a deliberate attempt, very recently, to rub and scratch the paper surface and further obscure the handwriting here. You can clearly see the broken surface of the paper. Fortunately it is high quality paper and there was enough left for it to be revealed.'

'Yes that is most interesting. Richard thanked her profusely for her team's efforts and for such a fast turnaround. He asked for the paintings to be stored for the rest of the week and called Fran.

She had found a little cafe in Covent Garden and he agreed to join them there. From this point it would be her job to do what she could, to determine provenance. He called Andrew, arranged to meet him on Tuesday and then hailed a cab.

He discovered his family in an underground bistro, engrossed in viewing the great number of photographs Emily had sent to Izzy. They had finished their lunch, and were sipping milkshakes. Richard ordered a long black, a pork pie and pickled onions, and asked for HP sauce. Fran looked at him with raised eyebrows. 'When in Rome,' he said.

'So how did it go?'

'Well of course I was right'.

'Darling that goes without saying, have you ever been wrong? Let me rephrase that. Have you ever admitted to being wrong?'

'No, on both counts.'

'Thought not. Ok give.'

Richard related his experiences of the morning whilst demolishing an English pork pie which had appeared for some reason with chips.

'So the work thought to be Freud is still in contention. Dare we assume it is by…?' asked Fran.

'Yes, the one and only Leon Scully'.

'In fact I am prepared to say so categorically. I believe it can definitely be attributed to Leon. I have always wondered why there seemed so few paintings of his wife? I mean there's more than fifty of her sister. I think there are just two we have come across so far of Nadja. I am prepared to go a little further and say this work is probably a preliminary painting for something bigger and even better.'

'So Darling where do we go from here, what's the next step?'

'Well the most important bit really. This is where we need to call on your research skills.'

'Let me guess. Provenance?'

'You got it in one. Now, any of you ladies like a chip?' Emily did not refuse then without giving it much thought Fran also helped herself.

Fran suggested she go back alone to the hotel and make a start on her laptop. Richard asked Emily if she would like to go to the Natural History Museum. He had discovered on Google there was and an exhibition called the '*The Tale of the Tall Emperor Penguin*'. He was concerned she may be tired but she claimed not to be.

'Then we will take the tube, and you can take lots of photos to show Izzy. "

     Brian Millard

'What's a tube?'

'It a kind of train that goes underground, so they call it The Underground'

'Cool'.

Fran decided to walk to Claridges. She watched as Richard and Emily strode off hand in hand, and when they turned and waved she did the same. Her little family we soon lost in the crowd on their way to the nearest central line. Emily took great interest in the underground and the escalators, and recorded everything diligently. They were soon in South Kensington and walking down Exhibition Road. Emily was in for a memorable experience. She had her tablet at the ready. She chanted, 'Mind the gap, mind the gap,' until they passed through the door of one of Britain's oldest and most respected museums. They could have spent all day in the company of the dinosaurs, but Emperor Penguins called. They took a cab home to find Fran typing.

'I've been a busy girl whilst you two have been enjoying yourselves. I've been slaving over a hot laptop and found out where Scully got married. It was of course the St Andrew Bobola Roman Catholic Church in Hammersmith. So I took myself to church. The priest was almost gaga, but he kindly looked through his records and, sure enough, there was an entry showing their names, their signatures and the date they tied the knot. And guess who was a witness and apparently the best man? Felix Topolski, no less. The old chap even pointed me to where they met, at the Polish Club. There was no friendly old informant there but a rather fierce middle aged lady in a twinset and pearls. It wasn't until I mentioned the magic words that she showed any real interest in my questions.'

'And what were the magic words?'

'Feliks Topolski.'

'Of course, silly me.'

'I'll have you know, dear old Feliks is revered in Hammersmith. There are pictures on the wall of him amongst the Polish airmen who took on the Nazis in the Battle of Britain. Understandable really because he was a real live Polish hero and did no end of good things for expat Poles in the day. He was already an established artist before he came to the UK, in 1935 – actually, he was commissioned to record King George V's Silver Jubilee, that's why he was here. But he made his name very early on in the piece, graduating from the Academy of Fine Arts in Warsaw. Then he joined the cavalry before going to study in France and Italy.

'Fran, get on with it.'

'Well, in the early fifties our Feliks was a busy man. As you know he had been an official war artist and painted scenes of the Battle of Britain and other battlefields. He was an accredited war artist to both Britain and Poland *and* also under contract, at the time, to Picture Post. His drawings became well-known when they were published by the magazine. After the war he was commissioned to document in paint the first meeting of the United Nations, he gained British citizenship in 1947. *But,*' She took a breath 'the demands of reporting on the world scene were ongoing and unpredictable. He could be off to cover any major disaster at the drop of a hat, anywhere in the world. He was a sort of war correspondent with a sketch book.'

'Darling, spare me the history lesson please'.

'Bear with me. This is all useful, Bacon was now living with his ailing mother in South Africa and Scully and Nadja would soon leave Britain for keeps. Bacon also spent time in the Middle-East and even longer gambling in Nice and Monaco. Imagine you were Topolski, he had offered to pick up Scully's painting of Nadja from Freud's studio at his request. When he arrived at the studio it was to find Kitty Godley distraught and preparing to leave Freud. She had had enough. The marriage was at an end. Freud was at the races betting on a horse he fancied. She thrust both paintings into Feliks's hands. Feliks had to leave the next day for India. But there was no Bacon or Scully to give them to. So in desperation he took the paintings to old Noah Assario and asked him to look after them until the artists they belonged to, could collect them. Look I know it is all supposition, but it fits, all I have to do now is prove it.'

             Brian Millard

'Fran we've had a busy day and Emily and I are starving.

'Well what I think had happened to Leo and Nadja was this. At the Polish club the news was that anyone seeking knowledge of the fate of their loved ones during the German and Russian ethnic cleansing, should come forward and make their existence known at NZ House. New Zealand had as we know granted asylum to 733 Polish child survivors but no one had bothered to tell Nadja. Leon and she hurried to the NZ Embassy and discovered that Kaja's name was on the list. This was the first timr they learnt that the children had been taken to Pahiatua. The children had been in New Zealand, would you believe, since 1944. The fate of her parents was not known. Anyway, as you can expect, Nadja was overjoyed at the possibility of seeing her sister again. They must go to New Zealand immediately, there was no time to be lost she would be reunited with her sister at last. If Leon had been wondering what had happened to his painting of his wife, he would have pushed it out of his mind. He made arrangements for them to leave on a BOAC flight the following week. It so happened this was the week Noah Assario died peacefully aged ninety two.

'And you got all this from a lady in twinset and pearls at this Polish Club?'

'Well fortunately she produced copies of the monthly news letter of the club from around the period and then other ladies appeared with a couple of their husbands with a collective age of about three centuries. They remembered Scully and Nadja's wedding because the reception was held on the premises. So by piecing the dates together a narrative began to emerge. The bit about the paintings going back and forth is pure supposition I admit but knowing what we do, thanks to your detective work with the wrapping paper, it seems perfectly logical. I am hoping to be able to confirm it tomorrow. Have you had an interesting day?'

'Emily and I have also had an educational time. Izzy has been deluged with images of dinosaurs of all descriptions and the Tale of an Emperor Penguin was most interesting. Well done Babe as usual you have come up with the goods. Can we please eat something now?' Fran tossed him the room service menu.

They were still eating when Fran's cell played a few bars of the Hungarian Rhapsody. She stood, crisp white linen napkin in hand and answered. 'Oh yes, thank you so much for calling back, I do hope you did not consider my request an imposition.' She walked into the bedroom, leaving Richard and Emily looking at each other. Richard shrugged and so did Emily.

'Well who was that? Richard asked as she came back into the room.'

'Emily and I have an invitation for high tea tomorrow with lady Felicity Assario'.

'How did you organise that may I ask?'

'I spoke to her aide, carer, secretary or something. Who manages her appointments, explained who I was and why we were here. I just requested an audience and voila.'

'Well Darling you never cease to surprise me.'

'And you are taking Emily with you?'

'That's all part of my plan.'

Just then Richard's cell beeped.

'Hi Andy,' he said. 'Yes a productive day I think. Especially now Fran is doing her sleuthing. We have opened up a few leads, still a little speculative but with luck… Yep. Ok, sounds great, just a sec.' He turned to Fran. 'Darling, how would you like dinner at Andrew's and Wendy's tomorrow night?' He turned back to his cell, 'Fran is nodding her head and she has a big grin on her face, now she's giving me the thumbs up and so is Emily. That would be lovely. Ok, look forward to it. Bye for now.'

'Another full day ahead,' said Fran. 'Now young lady the sooner you are in bed the better. I'll come in to tuck you up after your bath and you can tell me all about the scary Tyrannous Rex, deal?' Emily nodded and yawned.

'You forgot the Emperor Penguin. Do you know why they are called *Emperor* Penguin, Mummy?'

'No darling, why?'

'Because they're the biggest and the cleverest of all the penguins, they're like the boss of all the others.'

'I see, so you could say they rule the roost, said Fran.' She stood stiffly with her arms pressed to her sides and put her feet close together. Emily did the same and they both waddled off in penguin formation to Emily's bedroom.

It was a slightly overcast morning on Thursday as Fran and Emily walked the short distance to Green Park underground station, located the District line and caught the tube to little Venice. They were there before they knew it, Emily an old hand now, warning her mother solemnly to 'Mind the gap'. They emerged onto the Regent canal walkway into a profusion of large trees adorning its sides and a myriad of moored long boats and small craft crammed along both banks.

The house they were looking for sat discretely in pride of place along a row of other Regency style buildings. The heavy door was opened by a thin woman wearing equally thin rimmed spectacles, a simple black skirt and a crisp white shirt. Her dark hair was pulled severely back and held in place by a tortoise shell comb. She ushered them into a foyer with a very high ceiling, a carved wooden staircase with a stair lift, a black and white marble floor and a spectacularly ornate hanging light fixture. She opened the door to a sitting room and asked them to wait. It was no ordinary room. It was furnished in the Regency style, broad striped silk upholstery and claw feet abounded. The walls were hung with an assortment of antique Persian, Chinese and Indian rugs of exquisite design, others covered the polished oak floors. Amongst the many paintings Fran identified a Monet and a Renoir. She was so engaged when Lady Herminie Assario appeared on the arm of her personal help mate. 'Thank you Elizabeth I can manage now but perhaps I will need that dreadful walker thing.' Skinny Lizzie, as Fran could not help thinking of her, disappeared.

Lady Assario held out her hand regally and Fran shook it carefully, afraid it might break, the woman seemed so frail. She thanked her for seeing them and explained she needed to fill in a little background concerning the business of the two paintings and their provenance.

'It is entirely my pleasure, my dear,' the old lady said. 'I am unable to get about quite as well as I would wish these days, so my social life is somewhat restricted. And thank you for bringing your delightful young daughter, Emily is it?' Emily nodded politely, on her best behaviour. One comes into contact with so few children, they bring such joy into a dull life. So Emily what are your interests?'

'Penguins,' said Emily.

'Well what a coincidence I have a penguin of my very own.' Emily's eyes widened. 'He's over there – perhaps you would like to bring him over here, he's named Percy.' She indicated a figurine placed on a chiffoniere. Emily went over to it and looked at it and then at Fran enquiringly. Fran smiled and nodded her approval. Emily carried it back and handed it carefully to Lady Assario. 'We have had Percy for a very long time. He is extremely old you know, at least six hundred years old. He has survived remarkably well don't you think Emily? He was carved from whale bone by an Inuit a long time ago.' Emily was transfixed.

'I was just admiring your excellent taste. I have never seen such a superb art collection outside of a gallery or museum,' said Fran.

Elizabeth came into the room pushing a Zimmer frame and helped the old lady as she took hold of the handles. She tried a few tentative steps. 'Thank you Elizabeth I can manage the ghastly thing perfectly now. We will be ready for tea in ten minutes please.' She waited until the door was firmly closed and said confidentially. 'As you can see, needs must. She never leaves my side. Overly protective and she can be quite insistent sometimes. I am beginning to rely on her completely. But you were saying? Oh yes, the collection. It is very much like living in a museum. It's all in trust, everything catalogued, valued and insured. Well not quite all, it seems the two paintings you are here to discuss have only just come to light so at present they are not included.'

    Brian Millard

'May I ask where exactly they were found and by whom?'

'I thought I knew every nook and cranny in this house but it seems not, Anthony found them hidden in a closet full of my father in law Noah's old stuff. I must have been in there a thousand times and never set eyes on them. How I missed them is a mystery. But Anthony just ferrets about for a little while and emerges wiping off dust from a parcel, proclaiming he'd discovered treasure, pleased as punch.'

'Why do you suppose the paintings were where they were?'

'Well it's understandable I suppose, considering how lackadaisical in his dealings poor Noah became towards the end of his life. Things were so different then, business done on a handshake or over a glass of port. The family, of course, built up their reputation as honest traders over the centuries, from the days when Venice was *the* hub for trade of this kind. But what began as a business exporting fine artefacts and furniture from the real Venice to the rest of the world ended prior to the Second World War and the holocaust. Noah could see where things were leading, so moved with his immediate family to England. He had extremely influential friends here and they no doubt helped arrange it all. He purchased this house and others and filled them with all manner of collectables and fine art. So the House of Assario continued in England. The client base changed very little, we simply carried on providing luxury products to our existing wealthy customers. Later, paintings played a larger part and trade in artefacts and carpets dropped away. Noah had an amazing knowledge of antiques and so forth but book keeping and detail were not his strong point. Even when Assario could boast a stable of top name artists, his accounting skills, shall we say, were rather casual. So you see it is possible, as his dementia set in, that he might easily have omitted a couple of paintings from the inventory and forgotten all about them. Noah was an extraordinarily generous individual with a strong moral conscience, his charity actually earned him a lordship, although, to be honest, his purchase of a tract of land in Scotland also played a part. Do help yourself to tea my dear and Emily would you prefer a glass of milk?' Emily declined but accepted a chocolate biscuit instead. Fran poured tea.

Fascinating,' she said, 'I had no idea of the long history of the house of Assario. I *was* aware Venice was a centre of trade for luxury goods of all kinds from all over Europe, from Turkey in the middle-ages, India and even Russia. I've been to the Jewish Ghetto in Cannaregio several times for research purposes mainly but latterly for pleasure. What *is* amazing to me is its history goes back such a long way, in fact for five hundred years or more.'

'Of course, but by the time my dear husband took the reins the company had already changed a great deal and diversified into other areas. Noah sired several offspring, mainly sons. They had no interest in the arts whatsoever. Their interests were rather more prosaic. Fortunately so because had it not been for their enterprise and diversification it is unlikely the business would have survived. The art side now is relegated to what Anthony likes to call a 'lost leader'. He is still keen to revive it and make it profitable again. My husband Edwin was the youngest son and probably best suited to continue the art side of the family interests after Noah passed away. But he was not his father, he did not have his charm and engaging personality, he had the mind of an accountant, he kept the books impeccably, dotted every eye, crossed every tee, he was meticulous in his dealings, honest and fair but he lacked the compassion and fun of his father.

'So your late husband is unlikely to have ignored a parcel containing potentially valuable artworks?'

'No Francesca, I do not believe he would. It does concern me. Actually I have taken the trouble to see if there is any written record in the account books from the late forties just to be sure'. Emily had not been able to take her eyes off the penguin sculpture where it had been left, in front of her, on the table. She reached out to touch it. She caught her mother's eye. Fran shook her head. Emily withdrew her hand and busied herself with her smart phone. Elizabeth appeared and cleared away the tea things.

 Brian Millard

'Elizabeth there are a few old accounts books on my bedside table, would you be kind enough to bring them to me please?'

'And was there a record of the paintings?'

'Well no there was not, at least as far as I could tell. But you will be able to see for yourself in a few moments, my dear. What a pity Edwin isn't here to solve the mystery.'

'You must still miss him dreadfully.'

'Nothing prepares you for it you know. Everything changes, everything. He was a lovely man, we shared so much. Oh dear, when your life partner goes, you must be grateful for the time you had together. But there was no warning, one minute I was scolding him for something silly and the next well- Ah here's Elizabeth. My goodness you have brought everything, they must be dreadfully heavy you poor thing, put them down here. It was only up to the end of the nineteen fifties I needed, I'm so sorry.'

'It was no trouble, Have you forgotten the time?'

'The time? What of it?'

'It's time for your medication.' Elizabeth whispered.'

Oh really, so soon, very well. Please Francesca feel free to browse through the books, maybe you will have more luck than I did. This will take just a few minutes but Elizabeth will need to check my vital signs and give me a little injection.' With help she pushed her walker towards the door and shuffled out of the room.

Fran immediately scanned through entries in the day by day accounts books. She could find no mention of the paintings in question. She idly picked up the book for nineteen sixty to nineteen seventy. The entries had been made in a completely different style of handwriting. Where the earlier book entries had been made with a thick-nibbed fountain pen in the cursive, calligraphic hand belonging to Noah, the more recent entries were made by his son Edwin, whose handwriting was distinctly cramped, spidery and devoid of any flourish or artistry whatsoever. She was about to turn the page when she noticed a tiny inscription in the bottom left margin. She had time only to register the name Topolski and a date, which was hard to forget, the 4th of July, American Independence Day. The door opened again and Lady Hermione shuffled in on her walker supported by Elizabeth. Fran promptly placed the accounts book back on the table, inadvertently propping it against the base of the statuette of the penguin. She stood up and walked over to the portrait she had noticed earlier. As she expected, it was by Graham Sutherland. She turned to Lady Hermione and said. 'Is this who I think it is?

'Yes it's my late husband Edwin. It was painted a long time ago now, by his friend at the time Graham Sutherland. 'He was very handsome then, don't you think?'

'Very.'

'Shortly after it was painted, they fell out over some trifling matter, and Graham placed his work elsewhere. Edwin was very hurt, well his pride certainly was, particularly as Graham persuade Francis and Leon to leave with him. Then the unkindest cut of all, Lucian also followed them. Edwin wanted to dispose of the portrait. But I stood firm and he gave it to me. It is precious to me now more than ever. You never know my dear. You must hold the one you love close and never allow anything to come between you. Never go to bed on a cross word. I take it you found nothing in the books?' Fran shrugged. 'Then in that case Elizabeth please put them back where you found them.' Elizabeth gathered up the accounts books and struggled out of the door with them in her arms. She turned at the door 'It's time for your nap. I'll be back to get you ready in a few minutes,' she said nodding pointedly towards Fran.

'It seems it is time for us to conclude our chat my dear,' Lady Assario said apologetically. I have enjoyed talking with you a great deal and especially meeting you Emily, such a well behaved young lady. Please give my kind regards to your husband Richard. We met at the Venice Biennale a few years ago. Edwin always spoke highly of him.

'I'm sure the feeling was mutual. I will tell him. Thank you very much for being so generous with your time '

     Brian Millard

'If there is anything else I can help you with, please call. I think Peter Penguin will miss *you* Emily, won't you Peter?' Emily waved to the penguin, held her cell phone tightly in one hand and smiling her best smile, shook the old lady's hand with the other. Lady Hermione Assario leant down and kissed her on the forehead. Elizabeth reappeared and showed them out.

They were at the tube station when Fran made a decision. She called the Assario residence and spoke with Elizabeth who put her through to Lady Assario. She apologised for bothering her yet again and asked if Lady Assoria would kindly check out the accounts book for 1963 and confirm if there was any mention of the paintings in the early part of the year, particularly for July 4, American Independence Day. 'It's just a hunch,' she said. Within half an hour there was a reply. She learnt that no such inscription could be found. The reason being that the page for July 4 1963 had apparently been removed, in fact, torn out of the book. Lady Assario was concerned and disturbed, she was sure Edwin would not adulterate an accounts book in this manner. She promised to get to the bottom of the matter promptly.

Meanwhile Richard was retracing his steps to Waterloo Station and the Hungerford Bridge. He had called in to the newly remodelled Topolski 'Memoir of a Century' Gallery the day before. It had once been Topolski's studio. Richard had been there purely because of something that had been nagging him. Why two paintings? He asked himself and why particularly Bacon and Scully? They were friends but it did not explain what the paintings were doing, stored together all this time by Assario.

Was Fran's theory correct that Bacon and Scully had painted Nadja Pasternak in Freud's studio and the paintings were left there for some reason? But if they had in fact then been returned to Topolski, was it possible that they had found their way to this very spot? On his previous visit, he had been impressed with the displays but realised it would all have looked different in the fifties. He had wandered around looking for places a parcel of paintings could possibly have been hidden. He had even asked an attendant if it might be possible to have a few words with the curator or whoever was in charge. He explained who he was and expressed an interest in Topolski and his phenomenal output. He learnt the curator was away that day and perhaps he might have more luck tomorrow. Richard had given him his card and asked if the curator could call him before he left at the weekend for New Zealand. He had not received a call.

He found the same attendant he had spoken to earlier and was told the curator was on the premises and he would let her know he was there. A pretty young Asian woman joined him ten minutes later. She introduced herself as Ming Lui. Richard introduced himself formally and thanked her for seeing him. He told her how impressed he was with the displays and presentation of Topolski's massive achievement. Ming told him proudly that the gallery had been opened, not so long ago, by Prime Minister Boris Johnson. Richard asked a few questions about the recent renovations, when they were started and how long it took to produce such an inspiring result. She was flattered. Richard then asked her directly if, in the process of clearing away debris and rubbish, a parcel had been discovered wrapped in Assario wrapping paper? He showed her a shot of the parcel on his cell. She examined it carefully.

'One moment,' she said, holding up a finger, and then tapped into her phone. 'Rodney, do you remember what happened to that old parcel we found in alcove seven a couple of months ago? Yes, that's the one. Do we still have it? Oh I see. No, no you did nothing wrong. You did the right thing. There's nothing to be concerned about. You *did* get a receipt for it, didn't you? Good, can you find it and bring it to the entrance now? Talk later. Yes I'm aware of that, it's on my list.' She turned to Richard. 'Well Doctor Symonds, It seems a parcel *was* discovered in the refurbishment. It had been stored securely in a dry spot and apart from a lot of dust from the building work seemed undamaged. It had been there for a long time. Hidden away in the area where Topolski worked. It was probably once a storage area because there were old art materials, canvases and so forth found with it. These items are now on show in the Topolski Process display.'

     Brian Millard

'So what exactly happened to the parcel after it was discovered?'

'Well our display manager contacted The House of Assario. As you are aware it was wrapped in paper carrying their logo. And Mr Assario came personally to collect it. He identified it as belonging to his company and took it away. Of course we insisted on a receipt. If I am not mistaken this is our display manager with the receipt now. A lean, bald, young man, pierced and tattooed, arrived, handed her a sheet of headed paper which she gave to Richard. Richard read the receipt carefully and noted it had been signed, witnessed and dated. The signature was that of Tony Assario. Richard asked if it was possible to have a photocopy made. Ming Lui nodded and asked Rodney to attend to it. He flounced off. She was keen to give Richard a personal guided tour of the show. He declined explaining he would like to return with his wife before they went home at the end of the week. He would take up her offer then. Rodney appeared waving the copy of the receipt. Richard, having made his thanks, left, amazed at his good fortune.

The family were united at the hotel shortly afterwards. There was a lot to talk about but as they were due to go to Andy and Wendy's place for dinner Fran had only time to give Richard a short version of her encounter with Lady Assario. Stressing how she had found her a charming and attractive personality, but she was concerned that her conclusions would upset her and she was not looking forward to telling her that her only son had most likely attempted to commit fraud. Similarly Richard explained where he had been and why. He showed her the copy of the receipt.

'Well that about clinches it, darling. Well done. Look at my hair. If you need me I'm in the bathroom getting ready for dinner. Emily why don't you put on that lovely dress we bought you at Harrods?'

'Harrods?' Richard gasped. 'Did you say Harrods?'

'In the sale, darling, don't panic But the one I got wasn't in the sale. Well you only live once. It will be worth it, you'll see.'

Whilst in the bathroom Fran answered a call from a rather distraught Lady Assario. A half an hour later Richard was treated to a fashion parade by both his loved ones and indeed he had to agree that whatever the garments cost, both his girls looked a million dollars? There was a call on the house phone to say their cab had arrived. The family sauntered down to the lobby of Claridges dressed in a style worthy of their surroundings.

It was good to eat a home cooked meal. It turned out to be a beef roast cooked to perfection, followed by a ubiquitous but beyond reproach apple and blackberry pudding with masses of custard. Emily and Wendy's girls soon became best friends. After dinner the three of them happily looked at the collected photographic works of Emily Symonds on her cell phone.

Andrew keen to hear what the outcome of their investigation was had listened intently to both accounts. 'So young Tony has been a rather naughty boy hasn't he? Can you imagine any other art dealer worth his salt not being able to tell a Freud from a Scully and then having the gall to try flog it off as an original Freud?'

'At least he got the Bacon right.' The question is what to do now.'

'Are we watertight?'

'How do you mean?'

'It becomes a legal matter now doesn't it? Fraud is a nasty word. It could have done us a great deal of harm if Christies had vouched for it.'

'Well as I said, we are still left with the question of what next?'

'Oh you two, honestly, it's simple,' said Fran. 'We obviously have to confront Assario with what we know and, more importantly, *prove* it. It's such a pity I did not have time to photograph Edwin's note about returning the paintings to Topolski. It is the vital link in the narrative of the crazy journey those paintings made. I was trying to find a way to tell you. I actually saw a note, in an account book for 1970, written by Edwin. It said he had sent paintings back to Topolski – to his studio on the fourth of July. But it seems the page has now disappeared, torn out by somebody. You don't

     Brian Millard

have to be Rhodes Scholar to work out by whom.' Emily was tugging at her sleeve. 'Yes Darling, Mummy's talking.'

Emily held out her cell phone. 'I was showing Bobby and Sam my pictures of Peter Penguin. Sam says he's just a silly statue, but he's not just a statue, he looks at you and his eyes follow where you go, look Mummy, see.'

Fran embarrassed, glanced at the photograph then looked more closely. 'Well would you believe it,' she said, grinning broadly and hugging Emily to her. Richard came around the table to see what the fuss was all about. The photograph showed an Inuit figurine carved in whale bone of a penguin and propped against it was an accounts book. In the bottom right margin was an inscription written in a tight, orderly but legible manner, which clearly read: "*Oil paintings x2 property of Francis Bacon and Leon Scully: Returned today to Feliks Topolski Studio, Hungerford Bridge. July 4 1970.*" Everyone gathered around Emily's cell phone and attempted to hug her, pat her on the back or tousle her hair.

Richard proposed a toast 'To Emily and Peter Penguin for providing the final piece in the jigsaw.'

'I'll drink to that,' said Andrew.

'And so most definitely will I,' exclaimed Fran. They all clinked glasses and toasted Emily.

'Thank you Darling, you are a chip off the old block, how clever of you,' said Richard.

Emily, suddenly finding herself the centre of attention and having received a sloppy kiss from her mother which had left lipstick on her cheek, hurriedly sought the protection of the other little girls.

Andrew declared he wanted to strike whilst the iron was hot and would arrange another meeting with Tony Assario to confront him with their findings early tomorrow.

Andrew had suggested he pick them up from the hotel after breakfast the next morning. The plan was to drop Emily off at his and Helen's place where she would be happy and safe in Helen's care and playing with their girls. He was outside Claridges on the dot of nine and drove them to The House of Assario. To their surprise, they found a Bentley parked outside the building, and Lady Assario being helped into a wheelchair by Elizabeth and a gentleman they did not know. They waited until the wheelchair and Lady Assario were inside, before entering themselves.

Tony Assario was sitting with his legs crossed and his eyes closed in one of his modern spindly chairs. He was dressed in a striped blazer and an ornate paisley waistcoat, pink canvas shoes and again sans socks. The unknown gentleman wished them good morning and introduced himself as the House of Assario's legal advisor. He was a partner in a well-known firm of lawyers. His name was Peter Abernathy.

'Let me begin,' said the lawyer. 'There is no need to prolong this meeting hence we will not waste time with refreshments. I have been charged with dealing with any potential legal matter that might arise today. Although, from what I gather, there may be absolutely no claim to answer. The paintings in question, those that were submitted for auction, were clearly done so in error. It was assumed they were the property of The House of Assario. This was a mistake, pure and simple, a misunderstanding. Also one of the paintings was mistaken to be by the late Lucian Freud, the other, it seems, was correctly credited and identified to be by Francis Bacon. The Assario family willingly concede these as facts and lay no claim whatsoever to the paintings.' His audience said nothing but exchanged glances. 'As you are aware Anthony Assario is inexperienced and new to the art world. He is a bright, intelligent young entrepreneur, full of new ideas, intent on making a change to the fortunes of the family flagship business. He is impatient and eager to prove himself. He freely admits he has made mistakes. But we ask what harm was done? Has anyone suffered any loss? Has anything occurred that is actually illegal? I think not – who in fact is the plaintiff here?' He turned to Andy. 'Mr de Malmanche, as the representative of Christie's auction house and someone who has had dealings with the Assario family

 Brian Millard

for many years — you must know them to be honourable and honest traders. Their reputation is as precious as your own. What say you sir?'

Andrew leant forward and looked the lawyer in the eye. 'Mr Abernathy this is not a court of law. We are not here to apportion blame or seek recompense of any kind. At least not at this moment, however I do not think the whole truth has been revealed. And there are questions we need to put to Mr Anthony Assario in the hope he can enlighten us. But it seems he has gone to sleep.'

'Lady Assario stamped her cane onto the floor 'Enough. I've heard quite enough. My son is a fool. He tried to sell something that did not belong to him. Then he tried to cover his tracks. He has admitted it, and he now understands that the good name of Assario could have been dragged into disrepute and a reputation, built up over centuries, seriously damaged. Anthony has been removed from his employment in the gallery, and new professional management will be employed. To some extent I have to accept some of the blame for his shameful behaviour. He has squandered every opportunity he has been offered. His dear father doted on him. I should have done something about it but did not. I do not believe he meant any harm. He has simply acted foolishly in the hope of proving himself to be more than he is. I can only hope this episode teaches him a lesson. Now if you'll excuse me.' She tried to make her wheelchair move but it was firmly stuck between the spindly table legs. Richard came to her aid. Her son stood and clambered up the stairs to his office. Peter Abernathy began to wheel the old lady away. She smiled sadly at Fran and said, 'Francesca could you and Richard kindly pay me another visit today. Shall we say for high tea at the same time as yesterday? And you young man,' she said addressing Andrew. 'Please have your legal people contact Mr Abernathy, that is should you feel there is anything for which The House of Assario have yet to answer. She touched Richard's hand briefly 'I look forward to seeing you later Richard.' They watched as the old lady was helped out of her wheelchair and into the back of the Bentley by Elizabeth and driven away by her legal advisor.

They were sitting outside a small cafe drinking coffee discussing what they had witnessed. 'Well that was short and sweet,' said Andrew. 'She really put me in my place. But you can't help admiring her style, can you?'

'She scared *me*,' agreed Richard.

'Well I think she's wonderful,' Fran said, 'she doesn't miss a trick. She's a real lady.'

'Actually Hermione was born in Golders Green, married Edwin who inherited the title from old Noah and that is how she became a lady,' said Andrew.

Richard and Fran looked at each other with raised eyebrows. 'We are expected in Little Venice. We will report back later,' said Richard, finishing his long black and standing up.

Andrew dropped the little family at the tube station and soon they were walking along the canal bank at Little Venice.

'This is really lovely,' commented Richard.

'You will like the house too.' said Fran.

They were ushered in by Elizabeth and left in the reception room. Emily went immediately to the figurine of the Penguin wanting to touch it but a look from her mother persuaded her otherwise. Richard went over to the Sutherland portrait of Edwin.

'Such a powerful painter, Freud owed a heck of a lot to him. Like Freud he was not after a likeness so much as the inner being, the very essence of the personality. This is so much Edwin.'

'I've always thought so.' He heard Lady Assario say behind him, she was hanging on to her Zimmer frame having been helped into the room by Elizabeth. I will never part with it.'

Richard turned and took her hand. 'It's been some time Hermione since we've seen each other.'

Indeed Richard, and in more pleasant circumstances. It was in Vienna I believe at your lecture at the Biennale was it not?'

     Brian Millard

'As I said, some time ago.'

'I did not need this dreadful contraption then.'

'None of us unfortunately are getting any younger.'

'My dear boy, you've hardly changed, a few grey hairs perhaps, makes you look rather distinguished. Don't you agree Francesca?'

'Why do men get more attractive as they age, it's not fair,' Fran said grinning broadly, 'but true, he's not too bad, for his age.'

'Daddy's dishy,' piped up Emily.'

'Yes he is, darling, definitely dishy.'

Elizabeth appeared with the tea tray, placed it down carefully on the table and helped Lady Assario into her chair.

'Thank you Elizabeth I can manage now. Elizabeth vanished as discretely as she had appeared.

'Thank you for pandering to an old lady's wishes and spending your valuable time with me once more. You must be keen to get home to your academic commitments. I was wondering, when exactly are you planning to leave?'

'On Sunday,' said Fran, we have a midday flight.'

'Then I did the right thing by asking you here. You see there was something I needed to say which would not have been appropriate this morning. I wanted to thank you for doing such a difficult job so professionally. Had it not been for your knowledge and acumen the reputation of a respected organization would have been put at definite risk. As it is it has been averted and no real harm has been done. For your interest, the culprit has been admonished severely and sent elsewhere, somewhere he is unlikely to create much trouble. He is actually on his way to Provence to learn about the wine trade at one of the family vineyards. Anthony is not a villain but he lacks commonsense. I mean he insists on dressing and acting like a rock star and prefers to be known as Tony. I feel sure he does it to prove he is his own man but honestly, I actually said to him, could he imagine Shakespeare writing a play called 'Tony and

Cleopatra'? I mean what's wrong with Anthony – a name from history and royalty? I'm sorry, it is so exasperating.' She waved a lace handkerchief in front of her face. 'Where was I? Oh yes. The second thing I wanted to do. I have a gift for Emily.'

At the sound of her name Emily looked up, eyes wide. 'I believe you have grown attached to a certain penguin in this room, have you not? Emily looked at Fran not sure how to respond. Fran, also unsure, simply gave her a 'don't look at me' look.

'Would you like to take Peter Penguin home to New Zealand with you? Emily's jaw dropped, she gaped in disbelief. 'I think he would be very happy with you and all the other little blue penguins. Emily gave her mother an imploring look. Fran nodded smiling. 'You may ask him how he feels about it yourself. Yes, you may pick him up.' So Emily did.

'Oh Lady Assario that is too generous, it is so old and valuable.' Fran said sincerely.

'My dear girl, please call me Hermione.

'But Hermione it is not a toy.'

'It is not a toy as far as Emily is concerned, that is certain, so I have no doubt Peter Penguin will be in safe hands.'

In any event 'old' does not necessarily equate with 'value'.

'But Hermione it is a precious artefact.'

My dear girl, I am more a precious artefact than it will ever be. There are literally thousands of identical carvings available and no market for them whatsoever. They are worth very little, probably much less than a couple of hundred pounds. My goodness, I use it as a paper weight. I would like Emily to have it.'

'Thank you Hermione we will treasure it.' Richard put his hand over Fran's. 'I think it's fitting, what do think Emily?' Emily bounded from her seat, embraced the old lady and kissed her on the cheek. Fran came over and did the same. Hermione stroked Emily's hair wistfully. The door opened and Elizabeth came in and whispered in her employer's ear.

       Brian Millard

'Well then, that's all settled. As you see it is that time again, I must take my medicine which at some point we all have to do. Please whenever you are in London, do not hesitate to visit again.

You can be sure of that,' said Richard.

That evening Richard called Andrew. Although his task was essentially complete, there were still a few loose ends to tie up. A decision was needed regarding where from now on, the paintings belonged. He felt guilty for leaving them as long as he had with the Courtauld Institute. The Francis Bacon was clearly the property of the Francis Bacon Trust. Similarly the Leon Scully painting was now the property of the New Zealand Government in the form of the Kaja Trust, of which he was chairman. He discovered Andrew was already on the job. Contact had been made with the Francis Bacon Trust and the legal work was well underway for the transfer and release of the Scully to Richard. He then called New Zealand and spoke with Judge Des Holland of the Coronial Court and gave him a short breakdown of what he had been doing for the last week and its outcome. He explained that an unknown work by Leon Scully had come to light and he might need to pull a few strings with NZ Customs to expedite its safe delivery.

Then it was Saturday and time for Richard to keep a promise he had made to Fran. He had a plan for their last day in London. Andrew collected Emily, who would spend the day with Bobby and Sam. Whether Fran suspected or not, she did not complain when he told her they were going to spend time together and enjoy London like tourists. It was a typical English day, so she thought it would be wise to take her lightweight raincoat and her sunglasses, just in case.

London in late spring – daffodils in Hyde Park, a boat trip on the Thames to the Tate Modern, lunch on the South Bank and dinner at Claridge's afterwards were on the agenda as promised. It was doubtful if Fran remembered Richard's initial bribe to persuade her to come with him to London, she took his arm, smiled and allowed herself to go where he led. The daffodils were in profusion in the park providing a brilliant display of brilliant yellow as they walked to the tube which would take them to the Tate Britain. They wandered through the various galleries for most of the morning. Admiring the Constables and the Turners, searching for personal favourites and being sometimes surprised at major works they had overlooked on earlier visits. They walked down to the ferry terminal and joined other tourists going to the Tate Modern. There is no better place to enjoy the river than from South Bank. And there is no better place to view the best of contemporary art than at the Tate Modern. They explored the exhibits, going from room to room, often in absolute awe from one collection to the other, sometimes challenged and given to disagreement as to the merits or not of some works, then agreeing to disagree. They had no chance of seeing it all and were soon footsore and hungry.

Lunch was beer-battered fish and chips from an Embankment cafe, eaten out of replica newspaper stained by vinegar and followed by a New Zealand style flat white, which came in for a little criticism, whilst sitting on a bench, watching boats moving slowly on the water. Fran stole a handful of Richard's chips as he was about to throw them to a bunch of persistent seagulls. He put his arm around her shoulders and they sat silently taking in the sun bouncing yellow light off the iconic buildings in front of them on the other bank.

'Darling,' said Fran, 'this is really romantic. Thank you.'

'It would be nothing without you.' She planted a kiss on his lips and put her head on his shoulder.

A few drops of rain fell, and the sea gulls scattered as they ran for shelter. Richard pulled his wife into the nearest pub. They stood at the bar, Fran with a glass of white wine in her hand and Richard with a pint of beer in his. They toasted each other. Then Fran pulled out her cell and called Emily. Emily was having a great time with the de Malmanche girls, she asked to speak with Helen who confirmed all was well and she should relax and enjoy herself.

    Brian Millard

She also reminded her that they were all having dinner together at Claridge's. Emily would come over with them. This arrangement was news to Fran, but as it was obviously another one of Richard's surprises, she made no comment.

'Can you manage one more gallery Darling? Richard asked 'If you are too tired it is no matter. But it is well worth it.'

'No problem, just as long as there will be time for me to have a long soak in the bath and put my glad rags on for the extra-special dinner.'

'Oh dear, it was supposed to be a surprise, was it Helen or Emily who told you?'

'Helen let it slip.'

'Then we'd best make a move, let's find a cab.'

A black cab dropped them off under the Hungerford bridge outside the entrance to the Topolski Gallery called the 'Topolski Century and Memoir of the 20th Century.' You could easily miss the discreet signage. Richard had called Ming Liu to say they were on their way and she was waiting for them. She gave them the VIP tour with a running commentary. They found it hard not to correct or elaborate. Fran was overwhelmed by the enormity of the artist's achievement which was made more meaningful by her recent delving into his personal involvement with Scully and the subsequent developments with the discovery of the paintings. She asked to see where they had been found. It was almost time to get back. There was a steady drizzle now. They hailed a black cab and were soon at the hotel where Fran made a beeline for the bathroom, shedding clothing as she went. It took a second for Richard to decide to do the same and join her in the bath. A few moments later he emerged wearing a towel around his waist. He went to the mini bar selected a half bottle of Bols, scooped up a couple of champagne glasses and went back into the bathroom, this was followed by the sound of a cork popping and a squeal from Fran.

Andrew and the three little girls were waiting, sitting at a private table in the L'Epicerie – set in Claridge's hallowed kitchens – where executive chef

Martin Nail held sway creating his exquisite dishes. Emily ran to greet them, excited to be up late and treated like a grown up. Richard and Fran were shown to their table and found they had front row seats to the culinary theatre of the kitchen. Wine was poured and Andrew stood to propose a toast to the House of Assario and their largesse. The party sat back, ready to enjoy the very finest of fine dining. It was to be a memorable meal and a fitting end to a busy week.

Andrew was at the hotel to drive them to the airport the next morning. They arrived in good time. Richard and Andrew shook hands and Richard promised to have their reports with him before the end of the week. They would, with luck, get together in the southern hemisphere summer. Andrew hugged Fran and waved as they disappeared into the departure lounge.

Once in their seats and the plane in the air it wasn't long before they were busy on their laptops preparing their individual reports. Apart from breaks for refreshments and meals this kept Fran and Richard occupied for most of the flight. Emily and the penguin watched kid's films and animated videos until it was time to sleep.

New Zealand Customs are vigilant. Richard had declared the penguin as a decorative carved figurine. It was viewed suspiciously by a pleasant but no nonsense customs official who finally called for advice from her superior. Peter Penguin was subjected to an undignified X-ray, an up close and personal examination and then fumigation before being allowed into New Zealand. They found Des waiting patiently for them at the barrier.

'It's Uncle Des,' cried Emily, running to him with her penguin held out proudly.

After Emily was asleep in her own bed, in her own room, Peter Penguin keeping an eye on things from her bedside table, Richard and Fran sat together on the couch in their sitting room, Fran with a cup of camomile tea, and Richard nursing a glass of Australian red. Fran put her too hot tea

     Brian Millard

down and leant into Richard, reached for his arm and pulled it around her shoulders.

'I was just thinking,' she said.

'What, darling, were you thinking?'

'I was thinking of fish and chips.'

'Sorry darling, the takeaway down the road will be closed at this time of night.'

'Fish and chips on the South Bank and the boats and that wonderful light, it was so romantic. And I can't help thinking about Leon Scully and what it must have been like for him to make the decision he did. Throw up his blossoming career in London and come back here, with two dependent women in tow.'

'He did it for love.'

'You have to admire the guy. He made it happen, didn't he? He created a lovely home, a sanctuary for them all and produced many wonderful works of art in the process. His sacrifice paid off. It was really was such a romantic thing to do.'

'And now there's another painting to be added to all the others, there may well be many more. I had just finished work on consolidating his catalogue raisonné when we left, now I've got to start from scratch.'

'Sometimes Richard I don't think you have a romantic bone in your body.'

New Zealand, 1970.

Leon Scully, his wife Nadja and her sister Kaja were living in a makeshift manner, in a large but broken down old cottage on a remote island in the Hauraki Gulf, north of Auckland. Leon had purchased the land prior to his departure for England almost a decade ago. In the three years they had been there he had renovated the cottage and made it liveable. It would be their home whilst he built what would be their permanent residence on a site a short walk away along the beach, on a hill commanding a splendid view out to sea. All the permits and inspections had been granted, and the building was well underway, the foundations finished, the basic structure complete. The remaining timbers and materials needed to bring it to completion were due to arrive by boat within a few days. Leon was a skilled carpenter and carver. His design for their new home, for the time, was revolutionary.

They had found Kaja in Pahiatua in the Polish camp known as Little Poland. They were appalled to discover that the trauma she had experienced in Poland had rendered her unable to speak. Throughout the ordeals she suffered she had been cared for by an older girl called Kristyna who had been a neighbour of the Pasternak family. She was able to tell them what had happened. She explained in a general manner how she and Kaja had witnessed the death of Kaja's father and then the subsequent death of her mother. Kaja had been left for dead but survived. But she never spoke from that day on. There was worse to come but throughout it all Kristyna had cared for her, spoke for her and managed to keep her safe.

When the sisters were finally united in New Zealand and the formalities completed, the day came when she was released into Nadja's and Leon's care. But the reality of being separated from Kristyna on whom she had relied absolutely for survival, was more than Kaja could bear. Perhaps she had hoped she would be allowed to leave the camp with her. She clung to her and shook her head, tears running down her face, unable to speak, she spoke instead with her eyes. Eventually, the older girl was able to persuade her that it would all be for the best and they would always be the closest of friends, she would come to visit her in her new home. Nadja held her tight and gradually Kaya's grip on the older girl relaxed and she let her go. Leon vowed he would protect and keep her safe for the rest of his life. Nadja was keen not to prolong their departure but believed Kristyna had held back the details of her parent's death in order to spare her inevitable anguish. She needed to know more and promised to keep in touch, perhaps there was a way Kristyna could visit the island, she would write to her soon.

     Brian Millard

For Kaja, then in her late teens, life on an island, accessible only by sea and well away from the troubles of the outside world, was bliss. The multitude of wild birds on the island became her friends. The birds knew no fear and in their innocent way helped heal her. She appeared to possess the ability to converse silently with them. She would allow them to feed from her hands, sit on her shoulders. She would walk, arms outstretched covered in birds of all species. She would dance and dance, her long, dark hair swirling, birds swooping joyously around her, following her as she moved. There was no need to speak.

Leon painted more prolifically than ever. He had ample studio space in the cottage. He sent work to a variety of galleries in Europe and America. He still had good relationships with galleries in England and sales continued to grow. He had begun a series of paintings of Kaja. What had started as references in his sketch book developed into larger, more ambitious works. Having started, it was not in his nature to stop. And as Kaja turned from being an attractive young girl into a beautiful woman the paintings grew in number and became almost an obsession. He determined he would not part with them. Kaja too began to paint. She painted her experiences of the occupation of Poland and its aftermath on a large wall of the studio. Leon watched her painting grow over the months, until it filled the entire wall. He made no comment and simply smiled his approval. It became Nadja's habit to entertain them, in the evenings, by playing her cello. Soon without any persuasion Kaja joined her on her violin. They would play chamber music by classic Polish composers, particularly Frederic Chopin. Leon would sit, nursing a glass of good red wine, basking in the glory of the music and the musicianship of the performance. Nadja wrote to Kristyna, and, within a couple of weeks, the cream boat brought her a reply. She sat on the jetty, legs dangling over the edge and read:

Dear Nadja,

I trust all is well with you and Kaja in your new home. It sounds idyllic. Thank you for writing to me in Polish. I have tried to forget about our country and what happened there. I write in English for practice, and, so as not to be reminded, please forgive my silly mistakes. Things in Pahiatua are improving for me, I have met a young Kiwi man who seems to like me and I like him also. His name is Trevor or Trev which he likes to be called. Well my Trev he has proposed marriage with me and I have said yes. He works on the land, like my father, in agriculture and has been to university for qualifications. I think he is a good man so you must be pleased for me. You ask me for the story of your Mama and Tata, and I will tell you. You need to know the truth no matter how painful this will be.

You will remember we were always friends when we lived in Feliksin. There was my father and mother and my older brother Fryderyk in the family. My family as you know owned a small plot of good soil and we grew vegetables. It was a closely knit community where we were, wasn't it? Everyone knew each other and we shared our lives. What we didn't eat we sold in Krakow. It was a way of life that had always been the same. We were always in and out of each other's houses. My little family were probably a little envious of you Pasternaks. It was only natural that Kaja and I became such close friends. Your mama was such a beautiful woman and your Tata a true artist. It was, in a way, an honour to live next door to someone whose work was sought after, only his violins could produce such a wonderful resonance, as did the oboes and double bass he made. His was a truly marvellous skill. We would listen in awe when you, little Kaya and your mama made the music. Your mama taught you well but then you seemed to be naturally talented. Well you really were the lucky one when they sent you off to London to study, You left just a few months before the Nazis came. Like I say, you were the lucky one.

The Szkop that's what we called them, cockroaches- because they were nothing but vermin. They robbed us. They took our freedom and we had to do as we were told. If you didn't, you would be punished, you could easily be shot. We carried on as best we could. Well, after Hitler's attempt to invade Russia failed, the Szkop began to leave. Things did not get better for us and I am sorry to say, it could not have been worse, because this gave the Russians a chance to move in. We did not

 Brian Millard

realise how good it had been with the Szkop. Those Red Army troops marched in with one thing in their mind. To take everything from us, everything we held dear and precious. They came in groups, sometimes they were starving and desperate themselves, due to being separated from their units, but even so, they were merciless. They killed and looted as they went. There was no way we could resist. All you could do was try to hide somewhere and hope. Well my father was a cautious man and he had learnt a lesson from the Nazis. He dug a tunnel from our cellar which was a kind of cold-store for root crops. The tunnel went a little way into the forest. It took him a very long time and was backbreaking work, my mother helped, as did my brother. The entrance in the cellar to the tunnel was hidden behind a wall of pumpkins, several layers deep. My father had nailed some thick skinned pumpkins to the top of the trap door. You could not see it in the dark.

Word came that the Russians were coming. We knew we should not let them find us. They could take as much food as they wanted and even if they burnt the house we would still be safe. So we used the tunnel. It was our secret, no one in the village knew of its existence, our friends and neighbours, even your family did not know. We were in the tunnel making our way to the forest when the Russians smashed down the door to our house and took what they could carry. They went down into the cellar but did not find the trap door. Then they went to your house. From the exit of the tunnel we could see what happened. My tata and mama tried to stop me looking but I was a curious child. They could not afford an argument or we would have been discovered.

Nadja my dear, I have come to a part of the story that will I fear will upset you very much, but you have asked me to tell you everything and I will. Perhaps it is for the best and what happened can be laid to rest. Not forgotten, how can we forget? But to hate as I have done is not good. So this is what happened to your family and to mine.

I watched as they dragged your tata out of the house. He did not resist and seemed to be trying to reason with them. The Russians laughed and threatened him with their bayonets. They knocked him to the ground and kicked him but he staggered to his feet. He was knocked down again by a blow from the butt of a rifle. He tried to get up again and he was hit again and again with the butts of their rifles.

Your mama came running out of the house shouting his name, little Kaja stood in the doorway wide eyed. Before your mama could get to your tata she too was clubbed in the face by a rifle butt and fell down into the snow. A group of a dozen or more Russian Red Army soldiers circled her. They fought over who should to be the first to rape her. Her clothes were stripped from her body and they took it in turns. Sometimes one would be pulled off her and another would unbutton his trousers and take his place. It went on for a long time. We could do nothing. We were so frightened we just looked on. In the end when it seemed she may have stopped breathing. One of the brutes threw his arms in the air in frustration and kicked her hard in the head then almost as an after-thought he drove his bayonet into her breast He had to put his boot on her to pull it out. Another soldier who must have been his superior came up and shouted into his face and struck him with the back of his hand. He shoved the soldier away and pulled a side-arm from a holster and shot your poor mama in the head. The bang seemed to echo a long time.

Kaja was no more than ten years old. I will never forget her screams. She ran towards your mama. 'Mama, i Tata, Mama, i Tata,' she screamed. But your Mama could not hear her. Kaja stopped, turned to run away but stepped into the arms of the Russian soldier with the revolver. He seemed bemused at first and looked intently into her eyes, he stroked her face. Then my little friend tried to break away, screaming again for her mama. She screamed and kept on screaming. The soldier took her by the throat and after a while the screams stopped. He had choked her and killed her with his bare hands we thought. He laid her lifeless body on the ground. A few of the other soldiers prodded her with their boots but she did not move. The Russian animals finally moved away, probably in search of other easy pickings. We waited until it was dark and we were sure it was safe. Your parents were dead. At first it seemed so was little Kaja. My father carried her back to our house and my mother examined her. 'She's alive,' she said.' Somehow she had survived. But my poor little friend,

     Brian Millard

she would never speak again. We took her to our house. It was a mess, they had taken everything. My father had left a side of ham curing in the chimney, the sausage that had been hanging from the ceiling, bread and preserves all gone. The cellar as well was almost empty, apart from pumpkins which are hard to carry, as you can imagine. But we cared for Kaja as best we could and she recovered, after a fashion. Perhaps some physical damage had been done to her throat or it may have been something to do with her mind. But she could not or would not say anything. She became part of the family, almost my sister. I spoke for her I understood her when others could not. I grew to love her as I think she did me.

The horror was too much to take. Nadja could read no further. Lying on her back on the warm, safe planks of the jetty she let the tears flow. The sun shone, a native robin fluttered to her side, head cocked, curious. When the tears had dried on her face she sat up and continued reading.

Nothing was the same again. We were always on our guard, looking over our shoulders expecting more visits from the Red Army. We were not disappointed. There were officers now and a kind of begrudging formality for a while. It did not last long. We were told we were to be resettled. We were to be moved somewhere safer. All lies of course. Deported, expelled from our homeland was the truth. We were made to board freight trains and climb into box carts normally used for cattle. They pushed us in together with the butts of their rifles. There was so little room it was hard to breathe. There was nothing to eat. What food there was fought over, the strongest always won. There was no privacy when you went to the toilet. The stink was unbearable. Old people and babies were the first to die. When the train had to stop for whatever reason, the dead babies would be dragged from their mothers and thrown out into the snow. It was bitterly cold, so we clung together for a little warmth. We lost track of time. My family managed to stay together for a while. But then, my brother, who was big for his age, headstrong and quick with his fists, did something stupid. The train had come to a halt at one of those water tower things. Guards with rifles patrolled along the track. They would open the sliding doors of the freight carriages a little, to let out the smell and for the excrement and dead bodies to be thrown out. The snow was deep and it was so cold that anyone trying to escape would be dead of exposure in a few hours. But my brother decided he would go and look for food. So he climbed out of the carriage and made his way to a pile of sacks left along the track. He was so stiff in his joints that he could barely stand let alone walk in deep snow. There was a shout and then a shot. My brother never came back. The train pulled out. It took a long time before it reached Siberia.

We were eventually fed and housed in camps. But it was so cold, so very cold. We ended up in a labour camp. Forced to work doing heavy manual work such as logging which was hard physical work. My tata knew about drainage and irrigation. He was able to work in a supervisory capacity and we worked with him for a while. But there was never enough food. I will never forget my mama slicing bread very thinly to make it go round. I used to dream of having enough bread to eat. It was always terribly cold. We were always cold and hungry. Then my father became ill. He caught pneumonia and coughed until his lungs burst. He died. After that my mama just gave in. We were told we were being sent to Persia, where it would be warm and where medical services and shelter would be available. But my mother was not strong enough to make the journey. It wasn't long before she too died and Kaja and I were on our own. We joined a group of the remnants of the Polish Army and travelled in convoy with them across Europe to the Middle East. Sometimes we travelled on foot, sometimes in vehicles or by train, scavenging for food and shelter as we went. And we reached a kind of safety in Persia or Iran as it is called now. We were looked after by the Red Cross. We had no idea where we would go from there or really what would happen to us. But we survived. Through it all Kaja never spoke a word.

I have hated writing this down, but you asked. Perhaps it's good, it has been a heavy load to carry.

You know the rest of the story and how we came to New Zealand. I have never left Pahiatua. But you have found your sister, who cannot speak her love, but will show it, I am sure. Please tell her she will stay in my heart for ever. Oh

 Brian Millard

With affection
Kristyna

When the new house was finished and furnished well enough for them to move in. The trio climbed the hill behind the house. They stood at the very top. Nadja took Kaya's hand and slipped her arm around Leon's waist, he put his hand over hers. They gazed out across the Hauraki Gulf. Wild horses, whipped up by the northwest wind, appeared and vanished, then reappeared, a bank of cumulous cloud gathered on the horizon, the sky turning yellow-green behind them. It would be another calm day tomorrow. The cream boat would call at the jetty in the morning with a delivery of groceries, there might be mail.

'Promise me something my love,' she said. Leon gently brushed the lock of hair falling across her face from her eyes.

'If it is in my power, whatever it is, I promise.'

'I never want to leave this place. I am happy here. Should I die first, promise me you will bury my ashes here, on this spot.' Leon put his hands on her shoulders, looked into her eyes and nodded slowly.

That evening Nadja prepared a sumptuous Polish meal using produce from her garden and fish she had caught from the jetty. As the evening drew to a close, in a room especially designed for the purpose, she and Kaja played Chopin duets for violin and cello. Leon was cajoled into accompanying them on the piano.

The very
thought
of you

England, 1946.

The boy had yet to reach his seventh birthday. He was standing looking out of the canteen window on the second floor of his school and it was dinner time. The school building was packed in tightly between factories. It was the middle of the day, the boy peered through the thick, almost impenetrable yellow-grey of a pea-souper fog. The only light came seeping from the factory windows and from a nearby gas lamp which created a dim halo of weak light in the gloom.

He stood with his back to the school kids sitting on benches, at long tables, eating their meals. He was a dinner monitor. His job was supposed to be to keep an eye out for any unruly behaviour. The job was sought after for the simple reason that when it became the monitors' turn to eat, they had the pick of the food left in the containers and instead of queuing and waiting to have the dinner ladies slop a ladle of this and a spoonful of that onto their plates, they were allowed to help themselves to as much as they wished and even have seconds. The boy stood shifting his weight from one leg to the other, his hands in his pockets. One of his socks was around an ankle, the other held up by a frayed, grubby elasticised garter. The narrow street and tall factories were pressing in on the school building. From somewhere beyond this circle of dim light the boy heard music which became more distinct as it drew close. The sound of a saxophone, an accordion and a harmonica playing counter-change to each other in gentle harmony grew louder. And then a male voice added its vibrato to the melody, the tenor voice sentient, unutterably sad and heart-rending. The boy recognized the lyrics of 'The Very Thought of You' familiar from the wireless.

A group of male figures emerged from the gloom. The singer, caught in a shaft of light from the lamp post, was dressed in a long, open great-coat over a shirt with the collar askew, sticking up at an angle, having lost a stud, or deliberately loosened. A white silk scarf was thrown around his throat and over a shoulder. His companions also dressed in overcoats that fell below their knees, gathered around the singer. Their heads were covered with flat-caps or berets, the exception being the singer, who wore a shiny top hat.

The boy could see he was moving slowly with the aid of crutches, one trouser leg pinned up above where his knee should have been. The harmonica player had lost an arm. One man held a violin, another a soprano saxophone and another carried an accordion. They shambled together into the faint pool of light. The singer stood leaning on a crutch, raised his arm to the sky, threw back his head and sang. The boy listened, entranced, until the song came to an end. The sadness, the sense of loss expressed by the music, coupled with the pathos of the scene almost bringing him to tears. The one legged singer removed his top hat and held it out towards the factory windows above. A few coins fell and tinkled onto the cobbles. The coins were picked up by the violinist with care and dignity and placed into a can. He saluted the windows above and stepped smartly backwards into the group. Then as a man the group turned and slipped together back into the enveloping fog. There was something about the group that spoke of the military, the habit of drill ingrained and not easily thrown off. A few moments later, the boy heard the saxophone start up again, and another sentimental, heart-rending tune came floating faintly through the fog.

What the boy had observed was the plight of a great many British returned servicemen, who had been wounded, shell-shocked, many damaged beyond repair. These were men who had lived through the nightmare of

 Brian Millard

war and survived, but, when they came home, discovered that the land for which they had fought had little more use for them. They had come home to a country incapable or unwilling to help them or reward them. Brothers in arms now reduced to busking for a few pennies on the street and having to sing for their supper. The boy turned away from the window. It was time for him and the other dinner monitors to eat.

Back in class, the teacher, a gentle would-be poet who had been deemed unfit for military service for one reason or another, read Tennyson's poem, 'The Charge of the Light Brigade', to his class of ignorant, generally unwashed, yet innocent kids. When he came to the end he tried to explain the meaning and context of the poem and asked the children if there were any questions. A couple of hands went up, one was from a kid wearing National Health glasses with a lens covered with tape, and the other belonged to the boy who had been looking out of the canteen window. The teacher, a little surprised, looked from one to the other of the boys. The kid with the glasses cried out eagerly 'Me, me Sir.'

Yes?' nodded the teacher.

'What's a 'league' Sir?'

'A league is about one and a half miles.' The teacher told him then turned to the other boy. And you have a question?'

The boy stood up and said. 'Out the window Sir, in the fog at dinner time, there were men playing music. Were they soldiers?

Well most likely, at least ex-servicemen, returned from the war.'

'Were they heroes as well sir?

'Oh most definitely, yes, yes, heroes indeed. That's a very good question.'

'Then why were they begging sir?'

The teacher looked bewildered. He had no words that could explain. No answer to give the boy. So he simply shrugged.

That evening the boy told his father what he had seen and heard and what his teacher had been at a loss to explain. His father was well in need of a rest from his work but he was concerned by his son's earnestness and persistent question of 'Why?' Why, he wanted to know, had these men been reduced to begging on the street? He needed an explanation for what he had witnessed.

His father though, was also unable to provide an answer and so after a few moments of thought, made a silly joke in an attempt to lift the boy's mood and make light of his seriousness'.

'Sounds like a 'bad salad' that bloke was singing,' he said, transposing the first consonants of the words. His father had never had to go to war, his skills had been put to good use instead, in a factory, welding aircraft parts deemed to be an essential industry. He put his arm around his son's shoulders then ruffled his hair reassuringly.

There is of course no answer, or at least no satisfactory answer as to why a nation should treat its heroes so negligently and carelessly. These men, given a uniform and a rifle, filled with ideas of glory and then sent naively off to fight and be killed, had embarrassingly survived. When they returned home, maimed in body and mind, they were at first proclaimed heroes, rewarded with words and had medals hung around their necks. Yet their need for a benefit to feed their families was virtually ignored. When they applied for assistance they were confronted with red tape and a seemingly heartless bureaucracy which paid lip-service to their requests. For thousands of embittered servicemen and their dependants, bewildered and robbed of human dignity, the reality was unemployment, homelessness and difficulty in putting food on the table.

In his bed that night the boy fell asleep, still confused, still deserving of an answer to his question of 'why?' But he held the memory of the man singing so beautifully in the fog carefully in his mind. The poignancy of the music haunts him still.

 Brian Millard

This is my second book of ten short stories. Although they masquerade as fiction there is often more than a grain of fact in there somewhere. In essence though where real people, places or events appear it is because it has have been necessary to make the plot work. What we know of historical characters in any event is not always true and should not be taken at face value.

BM